NEVER JUST FRIENDS

LILY CRAIG

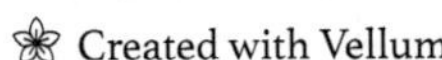
Created with Vellum

PROLOGUE

One Year Ago - Age 24

Georgie woke on the couch, Madelyn's words fresh in her mind.

"Don't worry,"—as if she'd have been anxious, not excited—"I would never date you."

So definite. Assured.

Not "I'm still figuring things out, and I'm grateful for your friendship." Not "my sexuality is new to me, but you're a dear, trusted friend." Not the words Georgie most desperately wanted to hear, "I'm gay and I think I love you, G."

She curled the blankets closer and winced at the memory. After knowing Madelyn for almost twenty years, Georgie had grown accustomed to self-protection. It was the only way she knew how to be the lesbian in love with her straight best friend: deny, deny, deny.

Some of that denial was internal, where she quashed her feelings whenever they arose and tried to pretend they didn't exist. Other times, Georgie rejected gossipy questions from Nadia and Hannah. They were her closest queer friends and seemed to think that just because they were a couple, they could spot others destined for the same fate. Denial was woven deeply into the fabric of Georgie's life.

But now, with Madelyn still sleeping in Georgie's bedroom, Georgie was running out of energy for denial. She had to face her emotions, and she'd spent half a lifetime trying to do the opposite. The truth had slapped her in the face last night when Madelyn came over and told her she'd broken up with her long-term boyfriend and was figuring out her sexuality, which at the very least was not straight.

And then Madelyn had said what would now be indelibly branded in Georgie's mind when she thought of her best friend.

Never date you.

Casually crushing every one of Georgie's long-held fantasies and hopes. Georgie shivered despite the blankets and realized something needed to change. Likely her. She couldn't keep living this half-hearted denial anymore.

Madelyn tiptoed out of the bedroom, walking quietly to let Georgie stay sleeping on the couch. Though Georgie was awake, she shut her eyes before Madelyn could see her; Georgie wasn't ready to deal with Mads, not while Georgie was still reeling with emotion.

Madelyn crept to the kitchen. Georgie heard cabinets opening and couldn't help herself. She opened her eyes to peek at Madelyn, who was wearing a simple oversized t-shirt and nothing but underwear beneath the cotton shirt. Her legs were long and toned and graceful like every part of her. When Madelyn turned to reach into the fridge, the faint lines of her breasts beneath the t-shirt made Georgie's stomach clench.

Madelyn was not only Georgie's closest friend in the entire world, but she was also gorgeous. It was all Georgie could do to keep gazing at the figure in her kitchen, allowing herself this one last look imbued with longing for everything she couldn't have.

Because now she knew what she had to do. To survive, to resist a complete implosion, Georgie had to move away. Her life in Calgary had been so shaped by Madelyn, so intertwined with her, that if Georgie stayed here, she'd never be able to move on.

She could find work quickly if she went up North. Welding was in demand with plenty of industrial oil-patch companies, and Georgie had honed her skills well.

If only she'd worked half as hard at moving past age-old crushes.

Georgie shook her head reflexively, trying to reject the impulse. Even consciously knowing that Madelyn wasn't interested didn't help—at least not yet. She sat up abruptly and stretched.

"Oh! Morning!" said Madelyn. Though her eyes were bleary, the color in her cheeks was as charming as ever. "I hope I didn't wake you."

"Morning," murmured Georgie. And she stumbled into the day, every feeling rioting against her newfound, definite knowledge: she had to get away.

She had to get over her best friend.

1

PRESENT DAY

Madelyn didn't have much time before she had to leave for the cabin. She'd been distracted until the absolute last minute with marking essays from the first-year History class she was a TA for this term.

In fact, Madelyn had barely made it to her parents' house for family Christmas dinner and a cursory gift exchange. Now, she knew she had to finish her marking and submit the grades before the deadline passed. But she also had revisions due for a paper she'd sent in to a journal recently. They'd made it sound like she could be published—really, actually published—if she just altered the paper a bit.

With this time crunch bearing down on her, Madelyn faced a dilemma. There was one last paper to grade, but the student hadn't actually submitted it until today. This student was normally attentive and engaged in class; it had seemed odd she hadn't made the due date last week. But there wasn't time for Madelyn to do both the revisions for her own work and the grading of the last paper.

Madelyn's student had emailed her this morning with the assignment attached, saying that her grandmother was dying. She apologized profusely and knew it was late but hoped Madelyn would understand. Except, for Madelyn, marking this paper would mean she had to leave her own work until later.

Grandmothers had a way of dying at inconvenient times in the school semester. The other teaching assistants had commiserated about this common excuse for lateness. Sometimes it was a grandparent, but it could also be a beloved aunt, uncle, or other tangential family member.

Madelyn wasn't a pushover, exactly, but with this student, her heart quivered. It didn't feel like an excuse. It felt real.

Moreover, she couldn't live with herself if she gave the student a zero on the paper for missing the deadline and just submitted the grades, closing the door on that entire issue. As much as it pained Madelyn to realize she'd blow past her own deadline, she responded to her student.

"Hi Jessa,

I'm sorry to hear about your grandmother. Don't worry about the paper's lateness. I'll mark it today and your grade will be available in the system when the course final has been processed.

Best,

M. Melnyk."

So what if it were a fake grandmother? Madelyn would rather have empathy for a thousand fake familial deaths than risk alienating sad, vulnerable students in their time of need. That was just how she rolled.

Madelyn marked the paper quickly and cursed herself while she packed for the cabin trip. With the grades submitted, she had just enough time to throw her laptop in its bag and tell herself she'd work on her paper's revisions while in the mountains.

Even today, she knew that was a lie.

Oh well.

She drove faster than normal out of Calgary towards the Rockies, letting her foot sink heavily on the gas pedal to make up for lost time. The trip sped by and she reached the National Park entrance booth surprisingly quickly.

"Hello, Bonjour," said the young man in a ranger's uniform. His unimpressed, half-hearted smile told Madelyn he'd had a long day.

"I'll take the Discovery Pass for one adult, please," she said. While she paid, she enjoyed the cool air on her skin, fresh snow drifting in the breeze. It wasn't too cold for a winter's afternoon.

She paid with a credit card and was about to accelerate past the booth when the ranger turned back to speak to her.

"Are you visiting for the day? Heading to Banff proper or points further out?"

"A cabin in the woods just out of town," answered Madelyn. She wondered if she'd done something wrong.

"Just a warning that we're expecting some weather to be coming in this week, a pretty big snowstorm."

"Oh!" Madelyn said, half planning the rest of the trip in her head already. "Don't worry, I've got winter tires on."

"All right then, you've been informed. Have a nice visit."

The young man returned to his seat and resumed texting while Madelyn zoomed ahead. Fresh snow might be nice for any outdoor activities she and the rest of the girls wanted to do.

Soon the ranger's caution evaporated completely from Madelyn's mind. She'd been thinking for weeks now about how she needed to talk to Georgie. It had been almost a year since her best friend moved away, and during that time, Madelyn had come to some surprising conclusions about herself.

This was supposed to be her time to address those conclusions while she had Georgie around in person. She pondered the matter while driving to the spot on her phone's GPS.

Madelyn had known when she booked the cabin that it would be fancy. The prow-shaped front windows were imposing, the thick timber framing inside classic in its lines. A beautiful spot, to be sure, but pricy. Showy. Everything that Georgie was not, in cabin form.

Yet Madelyn had felt the cabin's pull when she was browsing listings on Airbnb weeks earlier. If any of the cabins or condos in the mountains were the right places to tell your best friend how you felt, this was surely the one. It had room for quiet, private conversations. A fire to snuggle up to if things went right.

And if they didn't... Well, Madelyn would have to deal with that possibility later. She couldn't bear the emotions that pressed in on her from all sides when she considered what Georgie might say. Down that road lay devastation of the kind that might ruin everything. So, Madelyn had to keep moving, keep her spirits up and think positively.

It was her only option.

Madelyn took the turnoff inside Banff National Park to follow a steeply graded gravel road that allegedly led to the cabin. Seclusion would be good for them this year, she was certain of that.

Every year since they'd turned 16, Madelyn, Georgie, and their closest high school friends, Nadia and Hannah, gathered somewhere in the park to share in this, their post-Christmas ritual. It steeled them for the outside world while keeping them in touch. What had started as an excuse to get surreptitiously drunk and avoid their parents had turned into a meaningful tradition.

Maybe now, this time, it would become the most meaningful trip Madelyn had ever taken. She was to arrive a day before Georgie, and then Nadia and Hannah would come down a bit after that. Ever since Nadia and Hannah's wedding two years ago, they preferred a shorter trip. A few days later, they'd all rejoin the world and its competing needs, but this time was spent with their chosen family.

Madelyn wouldn't have it any other way. As she bumped along the gravel road, her car's splash guard scraping on the bottom from where she'd damaged it last year, she found herself grinning. The snow was thick and picturesque. Her back seat was loaded with groceries for the meals they'd cook together. And the trunk had boxes of beer, rum, and Bailey's for the in-between times they weren't hiking, skiing, or eating.

It was taking longer than she expected to find the place, though. The listing had claimed it was a thirty-minute drive from the town of Banff, but Madelyn suspected that was taking some serious liberties with road safety. She'd passed the more popular turnoffs to attractions where tourists flocked all year round. Now it was just her, the road, and a gradual sinking sensation that maybe she'd taken a wrong turn.

Five minutes after Madelyn made a promise with herself to turn back in ten if she hadn't found it, a sign appeared on the bumpy horizon. She revved the Pontiac's engine to climb the hill to read it.

Miller's Canyon Lodge it said, in faded letters that appeared to have been hand drawn.

"This is the start to a horror movie," Madelyn said to

herself. As if speaking the words out loud dispelled her fears.

Luckily, no chainsaw-wielding stranger jumped from the forest while she crept around the bend to head in the lodge's direction. Her music continued to pump pop-heavy beats into the otherwise soft and snowy environment. And while Madelyn thanked herself for remembering to put on her winter tires before the drive out, she nearly missed the final turnoff.

A narrow dirt pathway lurked on the right side of the road, nestled between thick pine trees. They nearly obscured the sister sign to the one she'd seen minutes earlier at the road she now thought of as major—at least compared to this one. If you didn't know you were close to the lodge by now, you'd drive right past it without a glance back to check if you'd missed anything.

Thankfully, Madelyn had been alert and hit the brakes, switched into reverse, and came back to the small entrance. She navigated a few stray branches that scraped at the exterior of her car like hungry arms clamoring for morsels of charity. And then she gasped when she saw the cabin.

It was bigger than she'd expected.

A lot bigger.

What had appeared to be a cozy four-person spot in the pictures online now loomed above her with space enough for twice that, maybe more. Madelyn was struck by the thought that whoever built this didn't want to be found, and yet they had a lot of space for their hermitage. She'd always thought that recluses preferred smaller, more quaint places.

The trees nestled in close to the building, which was grand though a little faded on the outside. There was a solid wooden deck on the front of the cabin, but even from the car Madelyn could see it needed to be stained. She could picture Georgie's silent disapproval as her eyes scanned the wood, probably mentally chastising the owner for being lazy.

If anyone was the opposite of lazy, it was Georgie. The thrill of thinking about her renewed Madelyn's sense of purpose and she drove the car the final few feet to a parking pad. Once the car was off, and Madelyn's joyful music had stopped blaring, silence rushed into the space.

Snow and isolation bred a carpet of complete hush, the kind that draws people to the mountains. But Madelyn hadn't been ready for just how quiet the outdoors was when she left the car, boot crunching on the parking pad gravel like a shotgun blast into the silence. A few moments of disorientation kept her standing there, one foot on the ground and the other still in the car.

She grew aware of the soft whisper of the wind in the trees, not a howl but a murmur. The car's engine cooled, clicking periodically beneath the background noise of Madelyn's breath. Any regrets she'd had about booking the space this far out of town were now cancelled by her excitement. They'd never stayed somewhere so wild before, so completely off on their own.

It was perfect—and not just because she knew how much Georgie needed a break. That first day or two with Georgie would be her chance, the moment she'd been steeling herself for all semester. But maybe, she thought now, Georgie would prefer if Madelyn held off for a day to enjoy the quiet first.

So that meant it was now 48 hours before she told the love of her life how she felt.

No big deal, right?

Madelyn shivered, noticing that she'd been standing by her car, lost in thoughts of Georgie yet again. She rotated her shoulders in a stretch meant to bring her out of her daydreams, and then she unloaded her bags from the car, one by one. The pile of food and liquor seemed insurmountable, but once the others arrived it would be consumed quickly.

It only took a few trips to bring the supplies into the cabin, though the first stop indoors had stunned Madelyn yet again. The antlers of deer, moose, and some creatures Madelyn didn't recognize but suspected were caribou decorated every available wall. The lone exception was the far corner near the fireplace, where a large taxidermied black bear reared up on its hind legs and roared in a silent rage out to the rest of the cabin. Rustic hunter charm overwhelmed the space.

Once she'd blinked her way through the shock of such an array of hunting trophies, Madelyn stacked her supplies on the wide butcher block countertops. They stretched from the right side of the main entrance all around the sizeable kitchen. She turned the satellite TV on for the sound of company, even if it were fake.

A local news reporter chattered about a contentious real estate development happening in the town of Banff, and Madelyn let the voice soothe her back into vacation mode. She hummed a song to herself that had been stuck in her head for a day or two but whose name and lyrics she didn't know. Gradually, the place started to feel more alive.

Groceries went into the large vintage fridge, which had a dried-up half lemon and several abandoned bottles of Kokanee in the back. Madelyn stacked the boxes of her craft beer neatly and then opened one for herself while she worked. It had already been chilled by the drive out of the city.

She explored the living room and dining room space,

one large area with vaulted ceilings and a fireplace that rivalled the size of the bear next to it. Logs were stacked next to the hearth on the side opposite the bear, and Madelyn suspected more firewood could be found outside. She thought she'd seen a lean-to in the pictures on Airbnb.

Gazing at the fireplace while sipping her beer, the holidays seemed real now. Madelyn pictured Georgie bending down over the hearth to start a fire—something Madelyn knew Georgie would be far more skilled at than she was. She'd wait until tomorrow for a fire.

She carried her bags up to the second floor, climbing the wide staircase in awe at the proportions of the cabin. It was spacious enough for a whole family to gather for a Christmas celebration, and for every member of that family to have their own room. Since Madelyn was first to arrive, she'd have her pick of the bedrooms.

She chose the smallest room at the back of the cabin. Its window faced the stand of trees nearest a rustic picnic table covered in snow. Small birds, whose feathers hardly seemed adequate protection against sub-zero temperatures, flitted around in the branches. On the bed, there was a thick wool blanket in Hudson Bay colors.

She'd claimed this space because she knew Georgie would be tired; it was best to leave the King-sized bed to her, allow her the comforts her daily life probably lacked. Affection surged in Madelyn's chest while she contemplated that bed, that room. Maybe she'd be able to share it. If she were lucky, if things went as she hoped they might.

Another sip from her beer fizzed in Madelyn's mouth while she unpacked her things, stacking them carefully in drawers while she thought about Georgie. Already, the daylight was thinning into late-afternoon darkness, an inescapable trait of Canadian winters. She wondered if there were television channels with movies available for her to watch tonight.

Closing the top drawer full of sweaters and socks, Madelyn bent down to open the bottom drawer. The wooden scraping sound was accompanied by a different, more distant noise. She stood up, alert. Her joke about the horror movie setting now rattled her nerves in earnest. All alone in the woods, concealed in forest and miles from the nearest town.

This was how scary movies started.

Madelyn stayed put, frozen in position, while she listened. Her heartbeat pounded her ribcage like a prisoner desperate for escape. Sounds made it past the interior hammering: someone was coming up the driveway.

The first thing Madelyn wished was that she'd taken a self-defence class like Georgie had suggested. It was a good way to dispel nerves, Georgie had argued. Even if you didn't think you'd need it. Then you'd know a bit more about how to handle yourself.

Barring the self-defence option, Madelyn rushed downstairs to lock the door. Maybe she could spot who it was before they got up the stairs to the deck and then she'd be able to tell if they were a harmless visitor or some weirdo coming for strangers in the woods. She had no cell service here, only a dusty landline in the kitchen corner that for all she knew didn't work.

Socked feet sliding on the wood of the floors, Madelyn raced along the lofted corridor, down the impressive staircase, glancing out the wall of windows to see the front forest and car tracks in the freshly falling snow. Footsteps began to sound their way up the exterior stairs, deck creaking under the person's weight.

She dead bolted the door and then shuffled to the side

so she could peer out the window. It was getting dim enough she wasn't sure who she was seeing, just a solid figure in a puffy coat with the hood up. Fur lining on the hood made the person look even bigger, and the thick sound of the mitten knocking on the door struck its way through Madelyn's nerves.

It had to be a good sign that they didn't simply try to open the front door, right?

She hesitated, unsure of whether there was a light she could turn on in the front that would allow her to see the person. Right now, the front peephole showed a person-shaped shadow looming in the dusk. Madelyn scrambled, flipping lights on and off until she found the right one.

The figure knocked again, double-time, the mittens dampening the blow in a way that somehow added more resonance to the knocks.

Madelyn found the right switch just before the person knocked again with one hand and reached into a pocket with the other. A cell phone, it looked like. Madelyn's eye darted back up to the scarf-covered face and recognized the eyes set above that plaid fabric.

"Oh my god!" she breathed, laughing at her fear now that it seemed superfluous. Madelyn unlocked the door and opened it, widening her arms to ready for a hug. "Georgie! You're here early!"

Her friend hesitated for a second and then stepped into her open arms. Their embrace rivalled what that stuffed bear could likely offer, fierce and warm and strong. When Georgie and Madelyn finally parted, Madelyn felt her stomach plunge like the loss was too much to cope with already.

"Sorry to surprise you," said Georgie, pulling down the scarf from her nose and mouth. Even without the covering, her voice continued in its characteristic muffled way, each word a soft mumble that only good listeners could fully appreciate. “Job let me take today off by surprise.”

"No, it's ok—better than ok... amazing!" said Madelyn, ushering Georgie inside. The falling snow had picked up its tempo, swirling in busy-looking eddies amongst the trees. Her heart fluttered alongside the snow, an inner tempest that Madelyn could not ignore.

Tomorrow she would tell her friend she loved her.

2

AGE 5

"Georgiana!" called her mother, voice cheery. The idea of her first day at school had excited Georgiana weeks ago, back when the notion was theoretical. Like when she played with her Lego blocks and imagined she could build the tallest building in the world with them. Kindergarten had taken up a fictional part of her brain and settled there sweetly alongside thoughts of candy and construction.

Now that the morning had arrived, and with it the need to follow her older siblings into the school, backpack in tow and lunch safely packed, Georgiana wished for nothing more than another year to be home, playing. She snuggled deeper into her blankets despite the growing warmth of the day, hoping that if she buried herself carefully enough, no one could ever find her.

Instead, her mother opened the door and crept inside, approaching the side of the bed with a cheerful smile.

"Wake up, sleepyhead! It's your first day of school. Time to get ready, sweetie," she said.

And so, Georgiana got out of bed, pretending she'd been

asleep for the last twenty minutes, and rubbed her eyes while the dread in the pit of her stomach strengthened. School was unfamiliar. Kids went there—big kids. She didn't know what she would do if she had to go to the bathroom, and when her older sisters had talked about the things they learned at dinner time, she'd always been amazed and a little frightened.

What if she wasn't good at school?

What if her teacher sent her home after the first day, carrying a note that said she was too stupid to learn and ought to be kept at home?

Georgiana said nothing, whirling in her private fears while her mother helped her into a light pink outfit, purchased the weekend prior to perfect her first-day-of-kindergarten photographs. The fabric was rough despite its feminine appearance and Georgiana squirmed.

"Hold still, dear," said her mother. Caroline Brewer was an efficient mother, having already raised two punctual, well-dressed children into little versions of herself. They were downstairs now eating breakfast while Caroline helped Georgiana into her dress.

"I don't like it," Georgiana said, the words escaping her like air from a balloon, involuntary and breathy.

"You look wonderful, sweetie. So precious," Caroline said. She had already turned away to pluck hair ties from her purse, tying Georgiana's glossy brown locks into pigtails.

The clenching feeling in Georgiana's stomach worsened.

Maybe she was dying.

At least then she wouldn't have to go to school. With a little cough, she excused herself to the bathroom. Caroline went downstairs to attend to the older children and left Georgiana frilly and itchy upstairs.

When Georgiana stood on the stepping stool and looked

at herself in the mirror, she knew she wasn't dying. But she almost wished she were. Anything would be better than plunging into the unknown world of school with this dress on. Her pigtails swayed jauntily as if they wanted to laugh at her woes.

Georgiana fixed her soft brown eyes on her reflection, and before she had time to pause and rethink her plan, she grabbed nail scissors from the drawer where she knew her father kept his things. A cut. Then another. With each snip, she took chunk after chunk of hair out of her pigtails. By the time her mother came up to check on her again, tapping on the bathroom door crisply, Georgiana had felled an entire pigtail.

Wisps of hair carpeted the area around the sink, clung to the ruffles of her dress, and floated down to the stool, floor, and bathroom rug in rings around her. When she moved to start on the other side of her hair, her mother's knocking grew more frantic.

"Honey, are you ok?" she asked, voice rising an octave.

"Just a minute," said Georgiana, saying the phrase she'd heard her father use so many times before. Her mother did not respond to her like she would her father.

"What are you doing, Georgiana? Let me in there, young lady."

Snip. Snip. The sounds of the scissors making their way through her hair was satisfying, and the sight of the pigtail growing short and ragged felt like a weight was being lifted off Georgiana's chest.

"I'm almost done," she said to her mother.

"Done what?"

But Georgiana was too focused on her work to respond, so the question hung in silence.

"Georgiana, done what?"

Caroline's rattling of the doorknob suddenly ceased, and a peculiar shuffling replaced it. Tiny scratching noises and a muffled word Georgiana knew you weren't supposed to say joined in. Then, just as Georgiana cut the last long strand of her right pigtail, scissors still held aloft up by the side of her head, her mother burst through the door, bobby pin in hand.

"No!" she shrieked, responding to the sight of hair around Georgiana as if it were a pool of blood. Caroline rushed to her and took the scissors from Georgiana's hand. "Oh my word, what have you done?"

I didn't like it, thought Georgiana.

The hair, the dress, the school. None of it.

Maybe now she wouldn't have to go.

Hope filled Georgiana while her mother fluttered around her, loosening the ribbons in her hair to assess the damage done, and then taking out a different, larger pair of scissors to try evening out the cuts. Downstairs, Georgiana's sisters clamored for lunch box snacks, a ride to school, any form of attention they could acquire.

It was fifteen minutes before Caroline's shaky hands calmed down, at which point Georgiana's hair had been modified into a clumsy bowl cut. In the Brewer family, hair was an emblem, carefully tended by professionals. It was not something you subjected to an amateur hand, except in clearly mutinous situations like these.

Caroline bundled the girls into their sleek black car and she drove them to the school, turning corners a little too sharply.

"Good job, Georgie," said Portia.

"You made us late," added Ariel. She frowned a pretty pout that failed to elicit sympathy from Georgiana.

"Girls, please," murmured Caroline, but her attention

was still focused on the road. She pulled up to the curb by the school and ushered them out, dabs of mascara streaked underneath her eyes from where the tears had spilled while she'd fixed Georgiana's hair.

Tried to, at least.

Georgiana felt the edges of her hair, now much farther up her head, and relished the breeze that flowed on her skin. Other kids were trotting towards the school doors, some waving back at parents to say goodbye while others were absorbed into the current of movement. Ariel and Portia left quickly, pecking Caroline on the cheek dutifully before they wandered into the crowd to find their friends.

Georgiana was left alone with her mother. Her throat tightened. She knew she was in trouble; her mother cared so much about keeping things neat and pretty. But it was her hair, wasn't it?

"Have a good first day, love," said Caroline. She hugged Georgiana and the trespasses of having shorn herself of her pigtails dwarfed in comparison to the terror of leaving.

Georgiana lingered in that hug, hoping that if she just kept on embracing her mother, the rest of the day wouldn't progress. She wouldn't have to show her face in a roomful of strangers. Wouldn't have to learn things or find out that she was the smallest kid. Her sisters always laughed at how tiny she was, telling her she'd understand things when she was older.

But they'd always be older than her, always just out of reach so that when she thought she'd caught up, there was new territory to enter.

Caroline kissed Georgiana's forehead and gently pushed her back, ending the hug with loving insistence.

"Time to go, dear."

"Do I have to?"

There was nothing to say, just a nod from Caroline while the school bell rang. Georgiana's mother led her to the classroom, spoke a few words to the teacher—maybe warning her of the haircut this morning—and waved goodbye as she strode out.

Georgiana was alone, except for the twenty other children sitting in their small desks. The teacher smiled at them generously, looming at the front like a beacon for their attention. Only, Georgiana couldn't stop staring around her, conscious of the way the other kids were smaller, just like her. Maybe being the same age as her classmates would be nice.

Her sisters hadn't prepared her for that possibility.

Maybe sisters weren't always the best judges of things.

A lesson on the letter A and how to sing the classroom clean-up song later, a bell rang. Recess. Georgiana moved slowly, like she was forcing her way through a pile of blankets to get out of bed, and when she reached the playground all the other kindergarteners had taken up the swings and sand.

She walked up to a boy near the edge of the playground whose name she'd heard and forgotten during the morning's lessons. He had a mop of sandy curls and a half-falling Band-Aid on his left hand.

"Can I play with you?" she asked, remembering the phrase from her mother's preparations the night before. If she asked, someone would say yes. That was how you made friends.

The boy didn't go along with the script, though. He squinted up at Georgiana, lips pouting while he took in the frilly dress, ragged hair, and plaintive look on her face.

"Why?" he asked.

She wasn't prepared for this, her stomach responding

with immediate, cramping panic. Georgiana had already started to back away from the playground when the little boy continued.

"Why do you have boy hair?" he asked. There was a hint of anger in his voice, frustration at being unable to categorize Georgiana by her hair or clothes. The dress seemed obviously, aggressively feminine, but her DIY haircut had dampened the overall girliness of her look.

That had been part of what she liked about it.

But on the playground, facing this disdainful boy's question, Georgiana wished she'd stayed home, pigtails intact. Or that she'd asked her mother if she could go to kindergarten another year, or at another school.

Apparently, the boy was friendly with a couple of other kids in her class, because he tugged on the shirt of a girl nearby and pointed to Georgiana.

"Is that a boy haircut?"

She wanted to shrink down into a Georgiana the size of an ant. Or escape to a garbage can and put the lid down on top of her new haircut. Something, anything to rid her of the stinging embarrassment from two, now three kids staring at her, completely confused by her.

It wasn't clear who started the cascade of laughter, but it crashed down on the playground within a few seconds of the initial pointing, so that Georgiana was caught on a pathway between the school and the jungle gym, visible from all angles as she was mocked.

She'd thought that her sisters were the meanest people she knew, but she saw now that she was wrong.

Other kids were all mean.

Terrible, horrible creatures who'd humiliate you, crush you on your first day of school.

Why bother going to school if this was what it felt like?

They were saying things now, mean things she was glad she could barely hear over the panicked roar of her own heart, bloodstream rushing wildly to flood her with adrenaline. Tears burned at her eyes, salty and ready to spill if she blinked again.

Georgiana stared at a point in the sky, wishing she could fly away. If her arms became wings and she flapped them hard enough, none of this would matter. Her hurt feelings would be left behind on the playground, scattered in a puff of feathers and wind.

Finally, she closed her eyes and let the tears fall, her ears still buffeted by the laughter of the group in front of her. While her eyes were closed, though, a soft touch of skin on her right hand startled her out of the vision of flying into the clouds.

"Hey!" whispered a girl with mussed sandy-blonde hair. Brown eyes stared at Georgiana from beneath a fringe of homemade bangs, and a smudge of what looked like chocolate icing was on the girl's cheek. It almost matched the color of her eyes, and the thought made Georgiana smile despite herself.

Chocolate eyes.

"Stop it!" shouted the girl, facing the laughing children on the playground. "It doesn't matter, because we're friends!"

Though the peals of laughter continued, Georgiana's chest tightness eased. Her embarrassment was now a load being borne by two, not one. The girl squeezed Georgiana's hand and tugged her away from the playground. They trotted to a bench near the back entrance of the school and now all that Georgiana could hear was the crunch of gravel beneath their feet.

Sitting down, they parted hands. Georgiana missed the warmth of that palm against hers.

"I'm a girl," she said quietly. "I cut my hair myself."

"Oh. I'm Madelyn," said the girl. She stuck out her hand to shake, clearly instructed by parents that this was the polite thing to do when you met someone. Georgiana mimicked what she'd seen her father do with friends coming over for dinner and shook back energetically.

"I hate school," said Georgiana. She wiped at the tears on her face with the edge of her dress, an inelegant motion that left wet spots on the fabric. Her mother would have been angry if she'd seen it.

Oh well. Georgiana was angry that her mother had put her in this dress, made her into a frilly spectacle when all she wanted was to wear the same thing she did every day: a blue t-shirt with a shark on it and the well-worn jeans she'd inherited from Ariel.

"Those kids were mean," said Madelyn. "But I'm excited for school. Aren't you? We get to learn how to write and spell and read big books. That's fun!"

The discomfort in Georgiana's chest swelled up again. Having to come here every day, to face those strangely cruel children who were so quick to judge her, it made her want to hide underneath her bed and never come out again.

"Maybe," she said. Even though Madelyn had saved her from the mean kids, she wasn't sure how much she could say yet. Despite being five years old, Georgiana had already gleaned that there was something different about her. Something that other children spotted from a mile away.

"What's your name?" asked Madelyn. When Georgiana met those chocolate eyes, she felt her stomach wobble in a funny way.

Madelyn wasn't like those kids on the playground. She didn't care who Georgiana was and she was nice to her.

"Georgiana. But only my mom calls me that. I don't like it."

"Do you have a nickname?" asked Madelyn. "My mama is called Radmila but everyone just says Mila. It's her nickname."

"I like Georgie."

"Georgie," said Madelyn. She spoke the name as if she were carefully committing it to memory.

In the moment of silence that followed, Georgiana realized she wanted to know this girl, to be close to her and watch her make these funny expressions and smudge chocolate icing on her face. There was brightness to her, drawing Georgiana closer without her even realizing it.

"I like it too," said Madelyn.

When Georgiana smiled then, the tears of a few minutes ago felt like an entirely different lifetime. Her mother had told her that going to school would be fun, would teach her things and help her make friends. Georgie hadn't believed her.

But now, sitting on the scuffed bench with Madelyn, Georgie realized that her mother had been right about one thing.

She had a friend.

3

PRESENT DAY

Georgie brought her bags inside the cabin. Though Madelyn offered to help, Georgie insisted on lugging supplies by herself. Some misplaced sense of pride, perhaps. Madelyn's mind latched onto the possibility that Georgie was trying to be chivalrous and that therefore she saw Madelyn *that* way.

The way where Georgie wanted to be gallant. As if she might respond positively to Madelyn saying what she'd been aching to say, for months now. Weeks of turning the words over in her head with careful reflection, imaginary conversations where Georgie's reaction ranged from horror to bliss.

For now, Madelyn merely appreciated the sight of Georgie hefting things up the stairs, her muscular thighs flexing with each step. Working in a physical job had been good for Georgie in more ways than one. Madelyn's body ached with heat watching her.

When Madelyn realized she was staring, she whirled back into the kitchen to start on dinner.

"What are you hungry for?" she shouted to Georgie. Madelyn's cheeks reddened with a blush she hoped would dissipate before Georgie came back downstairs for the next bag.

"What do you got?" came the reply from a bedroom upstairs.

"Tofu for scrambles, quinoa salad, a frozen lasagna, chicken pot pies I can reheat, more beer than I think we can physically consume during a year, let alone this trip. Steaks, some walleye my brother caught in the summer up North, sandwich stuff—"

"Steak!" interrupted Georgie, practically shouting the word with glee. "Say no more. Steak and beer sound like fucking heaven right now."

"Steak it is," said Madelyn. She took the meat out of the fridge, unpacking it from the butcher's paper with reverence. Though she wasn't normally a careful cook, she wanted this meal to knock Georgie's socks off.

Maybe other pieces of clothing too, she thought, and then blushed again. This time Georgie was walking towards the kitchen island and saw the expression. She misinterpreted it as a flustered response to the task of cooking.

"Hey, I can help," said Georgie. Before Madelyn could protest, Georgie came around the island and sidled up to her, gently touching the small of Madelyn's back to get her to move so she could reach for a pot.

"Potatoes good?" asked Georgie while she brandished the pot.

Madelyn's nerve endings tingled at Georgie's touch, a warm glow radiating from where her fingers had been on Madelyn's back. Madelyn's mind couldn't steady itself to respond, so she smiled, blinking vacantly for a second. Then she remembered where she was and nodded.

Her throat was scratchy now, hoarse with the rush of feeling that Georgie had unwittingly conjured.

"Sure," said Madelyn. Georgie rummaged through a cupboard to find the potatoes, taking out a cutting board shortly after. She started chopping the potatoes into rough cubes, moving with decisive strength. It was all Madelyn could do not to stare at those hands, willing them to come back to Madelyn's body and linger awhile.

"So how's life?" she said, clearing her throat. She seasoned the steaks and got out a cast iron pan from the lower part of the island. The snow was coming down too heavily outside for them to use the barbecue, and besides, the thing looked ancient. Who knew if it even had propane inside?

Madelyn was hyperaware of Georgie's presence, acutely embarrassed by the mundane nature of her question. She wanted to ask much deeper things, but the surprise of Georgie's arrival had shocked her into an unexpected state. Words were hard to find, and so was confidence.

Georgie shrugged, her head tilting to the side. She'd taken off the heavy overcoat and dusted snow from her lashes, shoulders, and face, but the beanie she still wore had damp spots where flakes had melted. Its red wool brought out rosy undertones in her cheeks.

"Not too bad. You?"

"It's ok," said Madelyn. She'd known Georgie was a woman of few words for years, and yet she'd never grown accustomed to how that taciturn nature made her feel helpless. You had to be careful to draw Georgie out slowly, to give her space, like a wild animal. The wrong question might elicit a half-hearted shrug, but then no further answers would be found.

"What have you been working on?" asked Madelyn. She

put the pan on the stove and began to heat it, adding a pat of butter that would foam with enthusiasm when the temperature was right. Georgie turned and put the potatoes on next to the cast iron pan, and her sleeve brushed against Madelyn.

"Same old industrial stuff," said Georgie. She'd trained as a welder when Madelyn was in undergrad. With the potatoes on the stove, Georgie opened the fridge to help herself to a beer. "You want one too?"

Madelyn was worried what she might say with alcohol in her system, but she nodded eagerly, thankful for the possibility of some social lubrication. In her mind, it had been easier to get back into a rhythm with Georgie.

In her mind, Georgie had never left.

Reality was much more complicated than that.

"Thanks. So do you like Edmonton? Miss Calgary at all?"

What she really wanted to ask was 'Do you miss me at all?' though Madelyn knew it was too forward. Being alone with Georgie again made her wistful and emotional.

Why couldn't they find the rhythm they once had?

Georgie must have caught the tone of Madelyn's voice shifting from polite inquiries to something deeper, because she looked up from the beer bottle label she was reading. Georgie had always liked knowing details like that, where the beer came from, what they had to say about the brew.

"It's been an adjustment, I'm not going to lie. But it's been a good year, too."

There. Madelyn had gotten multiple sentences out of Georgie at once. Whether it was the whirling snow outside creating a feeling of stronger intimacy, or the subtle influence of sipping the beer, she didn't care. All she wanted was for Georgie to look her in the eye and tell her everything about the past year.

It had been eleven months since Georgie moved to Edmonton, and Madelyn still remembered the morning when she woke and knew her friend no longer lived in the same city as her.

'I didn't want you to leave,' she'd wanted to say. But you couldn't force people to do things contrary to their needs. Madelyn still felt sadness every morning when she woke up, knowing her closest confidant lived hours away.

"I'm happy to hear it's been good," Madelyn said. Had she taken too long to respond? She couldn't tell. She and Georgie sipped at their beers, taking larger swigs now.

When the butter reached the right temperature, Madelyn turned to sear the steaks. The sizzling sound was deeply satisfying; she spooned the butter over the meat while she worked, waiting for the oven to pre-heat to the right temperature for the final stage of cooking. Already, a delicious smell wafted throughout the cabin.

"You still liking your job?" asked Georgie.

Madelyn turned to nod and a pop of the searing steak fat splattered onto her bare skin.

"Ouch!" she said, pulling back from the stove. Within an instant, Georgie had gotten off the bar stool and come around the island to Madelyn. She held Madelyn's arm and checked for a burn.

How could they be so close together now and yet not have breached the unspoken barrier between them?

Madelyn's skin tingled more from the gentle touch of Georgie's fingers on her arm than from the burn, but Georgie insisted on getting Band-Aids from her truck's first aid kit. Madelyn put the pan into the pre-heated oven while she waited. Near the door, Georgie threw on a coat and mittens, stuffed her feet into her boots, and ventured outside.

The gusting wind that met her surprised them both.

"Woah, it's really coming down out there," said Georgie. Her scarf muffled her voice slightly, but Madelyn could still discern the words. They were the same ones she herself had thought when she saw the depths of snow outside, the drifts piling near the cabin in uneven patches depending on the patterns of wind and shelter.

Even though it was dark, the eddies of snow still falling were visible against the light emanating from the cabin.

"Be careful," said Madelyn. She hadn't meant to, but the words slipped out before she could reconsider. If Georgie stumbled, or hit her head, Madelyn would regret not expressing worry. Georgie just nodded and waded into the snow.

The chill ran through the cabin after Georgie closed the door, an invisible tsunami of frigid air. While Madelyn shivered, she sidled up closer to the hot oven, trying to combat the goosebumps that prickled her skin in response to the draft. She heard the crunching of Georgie's footsteps cross the cabin deck and descend the staircase, and then the softer sounds of Georgie making her way to her vehicle.

If it were to snow this hard all night, would the others be able to get there? Madelyn thought she'd seen a seasonal closure sign near the start of the road to the cabin, and if there were enough snow, she wasn't sure the narrow gravel passage would be cleared quickly. If at all.

Though the prospect of being snowed in, adrift, miles from friends, family, and civilization should have been terrifying, Madelyn's chest warmed with an illogical spark of hope. She and Georgie would be together. At least they'd have that, a kind of intimacy.

Georgie's boots stomping their way back to the front door interrupted Madelyn's selfish hopes. The face that greeted her was dusted with snow and flushed from cold and exertion. Despite herself, Madelyn went over to help brush the flakes off Georgie's shoulders.

"It's ok," said Georgie gruffly.

Madelyn paused. Of course it was. Yet she was moved as if by an invisible force to draw closer to Georgie, to look up at her rosy face. Tiny beads of moisture gathered on Georgie's eyelashes where snowflakes had fallen during her expedition outside.

Dark eyes stared down at Madelyn, Georgie's stormy irises an enigma as always.

Madelyn cleared her throat and stepped back.

"Sorry," she mumbled.

Had things always been this awkward between them? It didn't seem like Madelyn could do anything right. She slunk back to the kitchen and pretended to check on the steaks, but really, she just needed an excuse to look at something. So she wouldn't stare at Georgie's back while she took off her outerwear.

Madelyn had almost forgotten that Band-Aids were the purpose of Georgie's stint outdoors, and when Georgie tapped on her shoulder she jumped.

"Didn't mean to scare you," said Georgie.

"It's nothing," Madelyn answered. But the racing of her heart said otherwise. It only accelerated when Georgie took her arm, holding up its soft underside to inspect the damage. A small welt of pink skin had appeared, a badge of cooking honor. The steaks did smell delicious.

Georgie's rough hands were cool against Madelyn's arm, slightly chilled from stepping outside even with mittens on. She unpeeled a bandage and put it on the welt, smoothing it down with a deft stroke over the surface of Madelyn's skin.

"Probably not necessary," said Madelyn. "But since you

went to all the trouble to go outside, I'll keep it. Do you even use Band-Aids for burns? Or is it like a salve that you need? Ointment?"

Georgie just looked at her, head cocked to the side at a gentle angle, and smiled. Madelyn's heartbeat pounded faster, reacting mutinously to her friend's charms.

"Ariel always said a Band-Aid is half about the covering up a wound and half about the ritual."

It surprised Madelyn that Georgie would speak so kindly about her sister, fondness evident in her eyes when she did so. Had they reconciled recently? There was so much to catch up on, and it seemed like there could never be enough time to do it.

"That's nice," she said, instead. The words were inadequate and sounded hollow. "Do you two, uh, talk these days?"

Georgie's laugh buoyed Madelyn's spirits, dispelling at least a few of the nerves skittering around her body. Then Georgie took another swig of her beer and sat on the bar stool across the island from where Madelyn was cooking.

"Yeah, we actually do."

"Wow."

"I know, times have changed."

Madelyn hesitated, glancing at the steaks and then back at Georgie.

"Mind if I ask what precipitated this change?"

Georgie sighed this time, and the wind outside roared dully. "Fuck if I know. She did help me pack up to move to Edmonton. And then she just started calling me to chat once I was there, acting like nothing ever happened between us to make things tense. Maybe in her mind, nothing did? But she's nice again—I mean, still WASP-y as all hell—but asking about how work's going, if I've been seeing anyone, whether I was coming down to Calgary for Christmas."

"Wow," Madelyn said. "So she's just going to pretend she was cool with you and not a bully growing up?"

Silence swelled to fill the room while Georgie deliberated. Her eyes never left the neck of her beer bottle.

"I don't know if this sounds stupid, but I don't really care why she's in my life again. Yes, she hurt me. Yes, she was a difficult person to be related to, but I'm glad she wants to know me better. Even if it's a little late."

The cooking timer went off and Madelyn ducked down to retrieve the steaks from the oven. The smell rising off the meat was almost unbearably enticing; Madelyn breathed it in deeply while she plated the food. While she finished serving dinner, their conversation resumed.

"I'm really happy to hear that, Georgie."

Their eyes met and Madelyn felt, for a second, like Georgie hadn't ever left Calgary. Like their friendship wasn't a shadow of what it once was. A connection still shone between them, no matter where they happened to rent apartments.

"I am, too." Georgie smiled. "How's your school stuff going?"

"My school stuff?" laughed Madelyn. "You mean grad school?"

"Yeah, sure."

Georgie had so far only nibbled at the potatoes on her plate. While Madelyn thought about how to describe the constant, pressure-filled stress of her days lately, Georgie cut into her steak. With the first bite in her mouth, her eyes widened dramatically.

"Jesus," she whispered. "Your cooking is even better than I remembered."

Madelyn batted her eyelashes in false bashfulness. "Why thank you," she said. But underneath her jokes of domesticity, her stomach leapt with pleasure at Georgie's obvious enjoyment of the food. She'd cooked something well enough to surprise Georgie. The feeling of pride that came from that almost emboldened her to talk more emotionally about things.

Almost.

"Grad school..." Madelyn sighed. "I'm not even sure I want to keep going. It pays so little, and the essays and course preparation and all that jazz are just weighing on me. Like it's hard enough to be trying to keep my head above water right now, you know?"

"No," said Georgie. "You have to stay in!"

The intensity of Georgie's rebuttal shocked Madelyn.

"You think so?"

"Of course!" said Georgie, slamming her palm on the island for emphasis. The wood reverberated with her blow. "You're the smartest person I know, Mads, and if you don't stick with it..."

"I'll miss 100% of the shots I never take?" Madelyn said, thinking of the motivational posters that had been plastered in their high school homeroom all those years ago.

"Something like that," said Georgie, smiling.

They ate in happy silence after that, and Madelyn didn't even mind the lapse in conversation. Despite spending the past year apart, despite all of her fears and worries leading up to this trip, Georgie was back.

Madelyn had her friend back.

4

Age 8

"Ten more minutes, everyone! Then out of the lunchroom!" cried Ms. Chamberlain, the Grade 3 teacher assigned to monitor that day's meal. She gave the children a warning for no apparent reason, which made Georgie's sister Ariel scoff.

"Doesn't she know there's a bell that'll tell us that?" said Ariel, tossing her hair over her shoulder in a gesture Georgie thought looked uncannily like their mother. She was only sitting with Ariel because their mother had insisted on them sticking together, 'just until Ariel felt better.'

Georgie hadn't wanted to tell her mother that Ariel seemed to feel just fine. She chatted her way through lunch, gossipy as ever, and simply didn't eat what was in front of her. But every evening when Georgie told her mother about Ariel's lack of appetite, Caroline's lips tightened, and she appeared deeply disappointed.

"She needs to eat," Caroline would mutter.

So Georgie was given the mission of making sure that

Caroline was informed of whether that happened. At the time, Georgie didn't recognize it as a kind of illness, just bizarre behavior on Ariel's part. It seemed like a waste of food.

On this day, Ariel's lunch was a rye bread sandwich with roast beef, a butterscotch pudding cup, homemade fruit leather, and carrot sticks carefully packaged in Tupperware. Georgie knew this because she'd eaten the same lunch twenty minutes before. Now she sat there, staring off into the distance at the bench in the corner.

Madelyn sat on the far side of the bench, hunched over a sad-looking paper bag. She'd eaten the small sandwich inside of it and now her shoulders drooped. Georgie and Madelyn hadn't spoken much this school year, but Georgie still found herself checking for Madelyn at recesses, wanting to make sure she was ok.

In the last few years, she'd learned that Madelyn was brave only when it applied to other people. For herself, she was often quiet beyond reason and seemed dreamily introverted if a problem came up. Georgie's lunchtime assignment to spend time with Ariel had been gnawing at her insides.

"Do you want that?" she asked Ariel, pointing at the lunch box of food. When Ariel rolled her eyes as if the question were beneath her, Georgie scooped the kit up and took it over to where Madelyn sat.

"Hi," Georgie said to Madelyn. "My sister's not hungry today. Do you want anything?"

Madelyn's warm brown eyes lit up with eager appetite. But she was too proud to say anything other than 'Sure' with tepid restraint. Georgie could tell she was hungry; it was obvious from the way Madelyn wolfed down the sandwich in huge bites, from her furious chewing of the fruit leather.

"Thank you," Madelyn said quietly when she'd finished eating. "That was really good."

"My sister doesn't eat lunch anymore," Georgie said. As if that were a logical explanation for their situation. "You can have hers when she doesn't want it."

Madelyn blushed and her dreamy expression turned to a frown. "It's ok, I don't need your help all the time."

Georgie felt shame tighten her muscles and then wondered what she'd done wrong. Wasn't helping people supposed to be a good thing?

"Ok," she said. But as she continued to sit with Madelyn, she watched Madelyn consume the rest of the lunch with a sort of resentful neediness and knew she'd done the right thing.

That evening, Caroline was thrilled to discover an empty lunchbox in Ariel's backpack. Georgie watched from the living room couch as her mother unpacked the bag, opened its zipper, and smiled a great big, beaming grin down at the empty containers. It was soothing enough that Georgie said nothing. Some part of her knew instinctually that to break the spell would be disastrous for both her and Ariel.

Silence it was.

Though Georgie had known Madelyn before, having recognized her as an ally in the fight against school bullies, they had never spent much time together outside recess. Now, though, they sat together each lunchtime, eating quietly while Georgie passed over Ariel's neglected food to Madelyn.

"Does your family not know how much you like to eat?" Georgie asked one day as she watched Madelyn scarf a sandwich.

"What?" said Madelyn. She seemed to sense a trap in the question, like its innocence was a front to conceal cruelty beneath it. Her eyes narrowed, sandy eyebrows densely pressed together.

"You seem really hungry is all."

"I know," muttered Madelyn. Her face had flushed with pink when Georgie asked the question, and though Georgie knew that she must be embarrassed she wasn't quite sure why. "My mom leaves early for work so I pack lunch from what's there."

"Where?"

"At home," said Madelyn. "In the fridge or just around."

Georgie wanted to ask if they didn't buy groceries often enough for there to be food, but something held her back from prying further. The obvious shame radiating from Madelyn's blushing cheeks kept Georgie silent. She'd never thought about whether other people had their moms make their lunches for them. She'd just assumed that was the way it was.

"Do you want to come over this afternoon?" she said, instead. Maybe she could show Madelyn the rocks she'd found by the hill in the park, ones that shimmered in the light with seams of sparkly crystal. Ariel and Portia didn't care about rocks, or lizards, or anything fun.

"Ok," said Madelyn. They continued to eat in comfortable silence, and Georgie's excitement burbled inside her stomach throughout the rest of the school day. She watched the classroom clock wind round through the minutes of each hour that afternoon. Quiet reading time was the worst part, with no distractions other than the words in front of her.

Miraculously, the time passed. Georgie shoved her book into the compartment beneath her desk and grabbed her backpack eagerly when the end-of-day bell rang. While their teacher lectured about homework assigned for Friday, Georgie shot a glance over to where Madelyn sat.

Was she as excited as Georgie? If she was, it wasn't obvious on her face. Georgie bounded over to the spot in front of where she knew Madelyn's locker was, and she fidgeted with the loose button on her coat while she waited.

Finally, Madelyn packed up her reading and shuffled out of the classroom. Madelyn's winter coat was too big for her, and the inside label had a name scrawled over it that wasn't Madelyn. Georgie's mother bought a new winter coat for each of her daughters each year, so the thought that a coat could be a hand-me-down didn't occur to Georgie.

"I just need to tell my brother where I'm going," said Madelyn, shrugging her backpack on top of the too-big winter coat.

"I can come with you," said Georgie. She didn't want to let Madelyn out of her sight in case she changed her mind about spending time together. Though Georgie's sisters were popular, Georgie knew that her own social prospects were much less promising. The consensus in her class was that Georgie was weird.

But maybe Madelyn didn't mind. She'd been a champion for Georgie in those early days of kindergarten, when Georgie's quirks had caused ridicule and embarrassment.

Georgie traipsed after Madelyn along the bustling elementary school hallway. They were headed towards the lockers for the Grade 7 class, as she could tell from her experience with her sisters' classrooms. When they reached the far corner of the hall, Madelyn poked her head around the open metal door of a locker where another sandy-haired figure stood.

"Sasha?" she said. The boy who looked down at them shared Madelyn's dark eyes, but unlike her small stature, he was already at a height that looked quite adult. A grim expression of resignation sat on his square face, and he stood with a slouching posture as if he were apologizing silently for his height.

"I'm going over to Georgie's for a bit. Is that ok?"

Sasha nodded, his face impassive, and continued to dress himself for the winter temperatures. Madelyn took his acceptance happily and steered Georgie down the stairs and to the outside.

"You don't need to check with your parents?" asked Georgie.

"Sasha takes care of me after school, so if he says it's good, it's ok."

Georgie still puzzled over Madelyn's unusual family situation. Her brother took care of her? Did they have to take the bus together or walk home, rather than having someone come pick them up at the end of the day?

Caroline was waiting for Georgie, Portia, and Ariel at the usual parking spot, the car still running to keep it warm while she sat. Georgie and Madelyn arrived after Ariel and Portia did, so the two older girls frowned at Georgie and complained bitterly when she let the cold air in with her.

"Mom, tell Georgie she needs to be faster getting ready to leave school," said Ariel.

"Or at least don't take so long getting into the car, Georgie," said Portia.

Caroline sighed and ignored the whining coming her way, and instead she smiled at Madelyn.

"Hello, dear," she said, turning around in the front seat so she could stare all the way down the minivan to where Madelyn sat in the back row. "I'm Caroline. And you are?"

"Madelyn Melnyk."

"I don't think I know your mom, Madelyn. What's her name?"

"Radmila."

Georgie didn't miss the judgmental look Ariel and Portia passed each other at that.

"Kind of a weird name," said Portia.

"Your name's weirder, Portia," snapped Georgie.

"It's pretty!" Portia shrieked.

"Georgiana! Manners. We have a guest in the car with us."

"Not my guest," said Ariel sulkily.

"Ariel! Girls!" Caroline used her most authoritative voice to attempt to quash the uprising happening in her back seat, a din of sibling rivalry. The sisters stopped talking, though Ariel and Portia crossed their arms and scowled back at Georgie, ignoring Madelyn completely.

They drove along bustling streets to the South-East suburb where the Brewer house sat, imposing, near an artificial pond. Though the suburb's marketing tried to paint the pond as a lake, everyone knew it was for storm water runoff, and its most popular use was as a repository for joyridden grocery store carts teenagers discarded. Madelyn's posture remained impeccably poised, but her eyes widened as she stared out the window at the houses they drove by.

Georgie knew that the houses on her street were large. Big families lived there, ones with children who played street hockey in the cul-de-sac or scampered around on the driveways shooting basketballs up at hoops over the garage door. She'd never thought more about the appearance of the suburb before now. It was more than just her home; it spoke about what her family was like.

"Thank you for picking us up," said Madelyn to Caroline when they hopped out of the minivan. Ariel, Portia, and

Georgie had all started walking up the front steps without speaking a word. Caroline, taken aback, smiled at Madelyn and said that she was very welcome.

Georgie noticed that her mother became nicer to Madelyn after that moment, opening the door with a delicate flourish and gesturing to Madelyn that she should take a seat on the good bench near the door so she could take off her boots. Usually, Caroline scolded the girls when they flung coats onto the bench and told them it was decorative, not functional.

"What would you girls like for a snack?" asked Caroline. Madelyn stared, switching her gaze from Caroline to Georgie and back again, unwilling to speak first. Ariel shrugged and went off to her room without answering, and Georgie could see the worry crease on her mother's face deepen in response.

Portia grabbed an apple and said she was good, thanks, so it was left to Georgie to answer.

"Ants on a log?" she said, staring at Madelyn hoping that she'd react positively. It was a little kid snack, Georgie knew, but she still loved it.

"Wonderful!" exclaimed Caroline. She threw herself into preparing the snack, ushering the girls into the den where they could play. Madelyn's eyes roved the sizeable built-in bookshelves, the marble mantelpiece and gleaming hardwood floors around them.

"Your house is really pretty," she said to Georgie in a low voice.

"Oh," answered Georgie. "Thank you?"

It hadn't occurred to Georgie that her house was beautiful; it was simply where she lived. Sometimes, she wished they had secret passages, or a workshop where she could collect more rocks and not get in trouble for having muddy shoes. But rarely did she ever look at the appearance of the place and assess its merits. Now, she watched Madelyn stare at the fireplace, and she felt a strange combination of pride and embarrassment.

"Snack's ready, girls!" called her mother, saving Georgie from having to think of something else to say.

While Madelyn ate log after log of celery, Georgie munched a few absentmindedly in between sips of chocolate milk. The peanut butter combined well with the drink, so she felt she was eating one of her favorite candies. Caroline watched the two of them eating and edged closer to the island.

"Madelyn, I can make more if you'd like," she said.

"Oh, they're really good. Thank you, Mrs. Brewer. But I had some of Georgie's extra lunch today so I'm ok."

Caroline raised an eyebrow at Georgie after Madelyn's comment, but she said nothing. The girls finished their snack and went to play and look at Georgie's rocks before Caroline had to drive Madelyn home. Georgie brimmed with pride as she explained that one of the rocks she had was what they called "fool's gold", even though it looked like it had real gold inside.

"So it's not really worth anything, even though it maybe could be if you didn't know any better."

"That's so cool!" exclaimed Madelyn. Georgie wanted to burst with happiness then, having not only found a recess friend but someone who'd listen to her talk about the things that her sisters thought were boring.

"Do you want to come over again sometime?" asked Georgie. Madelyn nodded vigorously. The two smiled at each other, a new sense of friendship forged in the eager silence. When it came time for Madelyn to go home, Georgie wanted to grab her hand and force her to stay.

After Caroline returned home from her errand, she cornered Georgie.

"What was Madelyn saying about an extra lunch, Georgie?"

She couldn't meet her mother's eye, staring instead at the pile of the carpet beneath her feet. "Sometimes I saw that Madelyn didn't have very much lunch. And she looked really hungry, so when Ariel didn't want her food, I thought Madelyn might want it."

"Oh, sweetie," said Caroline. "That's very kind of you."

"Did I do something wrong?" Shame was building inside Georgie, condensing the feeling of her blood pumping through veins so that she wondered if her heart might explode from the effort of keeping her alive.

"No, Georgie. You were being a good person trying to help your friend. It sounds like Madelyn's family might not have enough for her to eat sometimes. I'm just surprised that Ariel's still not eating properly, that's all."

In the pause that followed, Georgie squirmed. She knew she ought to have told her mother that Ariel wasn't eating her lunch, but she didn't understand the sadness blooming on her mother's face. It rained down from her brow over her soft blue eyes and on to the delicate cupid's bow framing her mouth. Georgie's mother was beautiful, feminine in a way Georgie already knew she was not.

Now that they were standing in silence together, she felt as if a moment had just passed where she saw her mom as an individual, a person who'd had a life before her children were born. It was the first time she'd considered such a thing, and she wondered why it hadn't come up before. Her mother was sad and though she couldn't help that, she wanted to.

"I'm sorry," Georgie said, finally.

The tears in Caroline's eyes never fell, but Georgie could see them wavering on the boundary of spilling. Georgie ground her teeth together and felt a rush of heat circling her neck—anger at Ariel for dodging her mother's questions about food every day, fear for Madelyn's confusing family, self-pity for being in the situation at all. This didn't feel like the kind of thing most kids had to deal with. But Georgie wasn't actually like most kids after all.

"Mom, are we rich?" asked Georgie. Her mother's faltering smile in response to the question brightened the mood considerably.

"No, honey. We're comfortable. Middle class, but comfortable." Caroline took a steadying breath and then shouted upstairs. "Ariel! Get down here right this instant, young lady!"

5

PRESENT DAY

When Madelyn woke, she had forgotten where she was. The unfamiliar wooden scent in the air confused her half-sleeping brain, and she jolted upright, searching for clues in the environment that could tell her where she was.

Log beams.

Trees outside.

Cabin!

She stood, stretching, and butterflies teemed in her stomach at the prospect of seeing Georgie again. Last night had been good.

At least, Madelyn thought it had been good. All her eager plans to tell Georgie about how she felt seemed silly in the context of Georgie arriving early. It wasn't that simple. Couldn't be.

Could it?

She longed to take Georgie's hand and kiss the work-toughened skin of her palm, meeting her eyes with an expression that somehow said everything she wanted to with words, but couldn't. Madelyn had finally figured out that she needed to be with Georgie, but the process of telling that to Georgie proved much more daunting than Madelyn's self-discovery.

Madelyn padded down the hallway, her socked feet light on the wooden floorboards, and when she reached the second-floor landing she paused, turning to the huge prow-shaped windows. Snow was still falling, piling onto massive drifts that changed the landscape outside completely. Everything was coated in thick piles of the stuff, from the heavily laden evergreens with branches bending underneath the snow's weight, to the front deck now covered by at least a foot of flakes.

It was incredible that something as simple as frozen crystals of water could join up to make this teeming, overwhelming vista. Madelyn stood at the second-floor railing and stared.

"I'm guessing Nadia and Hannah won't make it," said a voice coming from behind her. Madelyn jumped, whirling around to see Georgie, fully dressed already.

"Morning!" she said. "And no, I'd think the roads would be bad."

"Shit luck," said Georgie. Her eyes twinkled with warmth that was surprising at this hour, Madelyn being about as far from a morning person as you could get. It appalled her to see anyone happy before noon, especially before coffee.

Georgie was wearing a flannel button-up shirt in a navy plaid print, the sleeves rolled up to reveal her wiry forearms. Underneath a homemade beanie that Madelyn had sent Georgie in the mail for Georgie's birthday, wisps of messy brown hair were tangled rakishly.

"Hey," said Madelyn, suddenly unable to think of anything but the fact Georgie was wearing the hat she'd made her, "you like the knitting I made for you?"

"It's cozy," said Georgie, shrugging. "And I guess we'd better figure out what we'll do for the next while, cause even if we wanted to leave right now, there's no way we'd be able to drive home in this mess."

"No," said Madelyn. Luckily, they didn't need to return to city life for at least a few days, but the gusts of wind pouring bursts of snow into view wouldn't have bothered Madelyn even if they had plans to leave. She mentally thanked nature for bringing her this surprising turn of events, for providing her the perfect retreat to get back into Georgie's good graces.

"You hungry?" asked Georgie, tapping Madelyn's shoulder to get her attention before she started to walk downstairs. The jeans Georgie wore had a dark wash, the denim thick but fitted against her toned legs. Madelyn nodded vaguely while she watched Georgie move.

It was funny. All this time she'd been close to Georgie, she'd never thought of her as hot. Kind, yes. Dependable, of course. And obviously, Madelyn had grown fond of Georgie in her friend's absence and realized her true feelings. But she'd never noticed just how devastating Georgie was up close.

There was a casual aura to Georgie that belied the intensity of her inner workings. She stepped along the main floor of the cabin with her hands in her pockets, shoulders slouched and posture lazy. Madelyn watched from the second-floor landing while Georgie took out bread for toast and set out the jam and butter that Madelyn had brought.

"Come down here," said Georgie, smiling up at Madelyn. "Creeps me out to have someone watching from up there like a Dementor or something."

"Dementor?" laughed Madelyn. "Do I really look that rough before my coffee?"

Georgie mumbled something under her breath that

sounded like a swear. She rummaged through a cupboard and took out the coffee, brandishing it so Madelyn could see it. Within a few seconds, the coffee machine was burbling away, its sounds magical to Madelyn's ear.

"Sorry, forgot we had a caffeine junky in our midst," said Georgie. "Come on down, the water's fine."

"Water? You mean coffee, right?"

"Yeah, yeah."

As Madelyn descended, her gaze never leaving Georgie's fluid movements around the kitchen, she noticed that Georgie's initial reserve was wearing off. When she'd arrived yesterday, everything had felt wrong, like a skipped beat. Conversation was stilted, any silence deafening. Madelyn had tried consciously to get back into a rhythm with Georgie, but it had improved the most overnight when the two of them were sleeping.

She didn't know how it had happened, but she thanked the universe for its mysterious workings.

Snowfall trapping us together for the trip, check. Sleep that scrubs away some anxiety of reconnecting, also check.

Madelyn almost couldn't bear wishing that the same luck follow her through her confession to Georgie, whenever she gathered up the courage to actually do it. If she told her everything and Georgie smiled and agreed with her, that would be the greatest gift.

They ate a casual breakfast, Madelyn feeling self-conscious in her thin t-shirt without a bra. She didn't wear pyjamas other than old shirts and sweats normally, but in these close quarters with Georgie, Madelyn regretted not bringing along a nicer pair. Something that made her look rested and cute. That might draw Georgie's eye to Madelyn's assets.

"What do you want to do today?" Madelyn asked, setting

down her mug of coffee. Crumbs ringed the plate in front of her and there was a dab of jam still on the knife laying across it. Georgie stared out the window, wordlessly taking in the blustery view.

"God," said Georgie, stretching. Madelyn glanced at those sinewy forearms and felt heat gather at the back of her neck as she admired how they flexed while Georgie moved. Working in the trades had honed Georgie's already tough appearance into one of utility, and it was damn sexy. "I don't know. Think we could go for a swim?"

Madelyn watched in surprised silence for a second as Georgie laughed at her own joke. It'd been a long time since the two of them had been alone, and perhaps longer since Georgie had been in a good enough mood to joke–about anything. Now she was laughing at the biggest snowstorm Madelyn had seen in ages.

Two could play at that game, thought Madelyn.

"Yeah, let's get out there for a nice sunbathing session and then cool off with a dip in the lake. You want to borrow my sunscreen?" she said, smiling. But it was a silly thing to say, and the humor in Georgie's eyes dimmed to an embarrassed grin.

“Yeah, I'd like to get outside. We've been cooped up in here for a while and I don't think that snow's melting anytime soon."

Madelyn shoved her embarrassment down and tried to ignore it, opting instead to smile while meeting Georgie's gaze. "Sounds great. Let's go for a snowshoe? The listing for this place said there was outdoors equipment in the shed out back."

The plan was easier said than executed, for the piles of snow had closed off the shed from the path to the back door. Once Madelyn and Georgie had finished getting ready,

Madelyn changing into warm clothing while Georgie washed the dishes, they stood at the back with the door open. Wind blew sifting snow onto their faces while they strategized.

"How deep do you think that snow is?" asked Madelyn.

"Only one way to find out," said Georgie, stepping down the wooden stairs and into the drifts on the path. She sank to above the knees and turned back to shrug at Madelyn. "Guess it could be worse."

Georgie waded through the snow, breaking a path that made it easier for Madelyn to follow. With the door shut behind them, warmth had quickly dissipated to a thin layer of comfort beneath their coats. Flakes still fell around them, and though they were slower than last night's deluge they showed no signs of stopping outright.

Madelyn was surprised at how walking through the deep snowy path quickly worked up a sweat. It had only been about twenty feet of trudging, but the thickness of the snow and unsteadiness of each footstep had sapped her of energy. Her breath steamed into the air in front of her.

"Door's snowed shut," said Georgie, pointing to the piles of snow in front of where the latch closed the shed doors. "You seen a shovel around here?"

"Is it worth it, though? It was hard work just walking here. Maybe we don't need to snowshoe today?" asked Madelyn. A shower of snow fell onto her face from a branch above them and she spluttered.

Georgie laughed, apologizing quickly afterwards. "Sorry, it's just that your face was so... shocked," she said, hand on her hip while she grinned at Madelyn.

Madelyn would accept ten more branches dumping snow on her if it meant Georgie would smile at her like that. She knew most of the heat prickling her body was from the journey to the shed, but part of it warmed her center, a source she suspected owed more to Georgie's charm than the toll of winter. She brushed flakes from her face but a few lingered on her eyelashes.

"Go on, tell me more about your desire to see me humiliated by winter. Is that why you wanted to get outside? Personal avalanches, just for me?" said Madelyn. She sidled closer to Georgie, unable to keep her enthusiasm under wraps. Her right hand nudged Georgie's shoulder playfully, as if it had a will of its own.

Georgie raised an eyebrow. "I don't need to see you humiliated, just taken down a peg or two. Soon you'll be Dr. Melnyk and I won't be able to laugh at a Dr. Melnyk for anything. Would be wrong."

"Not true," murmured Madelyn, but the mood had already shifted. Gone was the fleeting cheer she'd felt bubble inside her. Now Georgie was already digging at the snow covering the base of the shed doors, lifting it out of the way with her mittened hands and kicking it with her boots.

Why did Georgie always have to make it seem like grad school would push them apart?

The Master's program Madelyn finished a couple years ago had awoken something inside her, a thirst for old volumes of knowledge that few wanted to read. Madelyn had always liked school, but graduate education had elevated that affection to flat-out love. She was excited to be in a doctorate program and wanted Georgie to be happy for her, too.

Though Madelyn's thoughts dampened her mood, she didn't let them stop her from helping Georgie displace the snow from the shed doors. They were getting closer to opening them, the left-hand side now jiggling a few inches further than it had before. Just when it seemed like their efforts would never be enough to get the doors open, the snow gave, and they pulled them back.

Inside, metal canoes lined the walls and fishing gear was strewn haphazardly about the back area, interspersed with a variety of sports balls. Madelyn saw cross-country skis that looked like they came from a garage sale in the 80s, and near the front sat several stacks of vintage snowshoes. They were the kind made of wood and strung with rawhide in a crisscrossing pattern like some bizarre tennis racket.

"Wow," breathed Georgie. "This looks a bit like its own summer camp."

"You don't see any newer snowshoes, do you?"

"These old ones will be fun. Let's try them."

"I don't know," said Madelyn. She already knew she'd say yes if Georgie pressed her. But she was also pretty confident that the newer style of snowshoes would be far more effective for their outing. No sense making today harder than it needed to be. She needed to conserve some energy for bravery.

Then again...

Georgie shook her head and grabbed a pair of the old school snowshoes, placing her boots on them and lacing them up before Madelyn could say anything further.

"How the fuck does this work?" said Georgie, laughing at herself as her mittened hands struggled to tie the rawhide straps around her feet and ankles. To Madelyn's eye, it appeared unlikely that the snowshoes would be particularly secure on Georgie's feet, but she knew no better way than what Georgie was trying.

"I have no clue," said Madelyn. She took another pair from the shed and tried to strap them onto her feet. She had no desire to snowshoe through the forest and then have them fall off, leaving her stranded in deep drifts.

With the best of their abilities combined, they managed to get snowshoes strapped to each of their boots. A few deep breaths later, Madelyn was ready to head out.

"Where are we going?" she asked Georgie, who was staring off at the thickly snow-covered road past the cabin. Madelyn wanted to walk along the forest edge rather than the road, the better to appreciate nature. "Here?"

She pointed to a passage through the trees that led from behind the firewood lean-to out towards a thicket of firs. It was just wide enough for their snowshoed feet to tromp along without getting caught in the underbrush.

"Sounds good."

Madelyn led the way, surprised at first by how much more difficult snowshoeing was from what she'd pictured. In her mind, she'd assumed that having snowshoes on made you able to walk on the very surface of the snow, light-footed and agile like Legolas from Lord of the Rings. The reality was that you still sank into the snow, just not as far as with regular boots. It wasn't long before Madelyn was breathing heavily and drenched in sweat.

The tallest branches above Georgie and Madelyn sheltered them from the snow so that fewer flakes managed to float down to where they walked. In that hushed environment, the only sound left to them was each trudging step, their own breath, and the rush of wind through the trees. Time passed in tiny increments.

"This is really beautiful," said Madelyn, finally. It had been at least ten minutes of reverent silence, the surrounding woods so vast that it felt wrong to penetrate that quiet with their voices, their human thoughts and woes. Georgie murmured a wordless agreement and then continued to walk.

They reached a clearing sometime after that, past a run-down fence that may have marked the end of the cabin's property. The small, flattened space nestled within the trees seemed sacred, just their own. Madelyn snowshoed her way to the side so that Georgie could enter the circular area to witness what Madelyn had just come upon: untouched depths of snow, bounded by impossibly large evergreens bending underneath the weight of their snow-burdened branches.

In the center of the clearing sat a young, spotted fawn.

Madelyn held a mitten up to her lips as if to shush Georgie, but she needn't have. The reverent silence with which Georgie approached the clearing showed she had seen the fawn. It was surprisingly small, curled up around itself to conserve warmth. Already, a layer of snow shrouded the fawn's coat—it had been sitting there long enough for a dusting of snow to cover it.

The fawn's soft brown eyes blinked at them, seeing the intruders to the space, but it was too timid to act without a parent. So Georgie and Madelyn stood there, wordlessly watching the creature breathe while snow fell all around them, coating the fawn in an ever-increasing cover.

6

MADELYN WASN'T SURE WHAT TO DO. THE FAWN QUIVERED IN the winter air for a minute, maybe longer, and though Madelyn was beginning to feel the cold, she wasn't certain she could turn back without feeling guilt about the animal.

"Should we take it back to the cabin?" she whispered to Georgie, afraid of startling the fawn.

"What? Why?" asked Georgie, staring at Madelyn as if she'd just suggested they teach the fawn to speak German.

"It looks cold, doesn't it?"

"Yeah, it's winter. I'm sure it *is* cold. But we can't take it back. First of all, how would we even bring it to the cabin? Second, it has a family. Its own kind, you know. If you take wild animals away from what they know, they're screwed. It'd die when we released it."

"But Georgie, maybe it'll die without our help," said Madelyn. She heard the rising sadness in her voice and willed herself not to sound like such a bleeding heart. Georgie often made her feel like it was illogical to have so much empathy, but Madelyn knew it also was part of what had drawn Georgie to her in the first place. They both felt deeply, even if Madelyn was the only one to show it.

"Tough," said Georgie. She turned back, facing the trail to show she was ready to leave. Madelyn's jaw clenched involuntarily, and a wave of nausea rushed over her. The fawn was helpless and alone in this storm. At least she and Georgie were staying at the cabin together—they had support.

"Really?"

"Yes, really. If we touched that fawn now, if we could even get to it before it ran away, its mother would reject it. We'd be dooming it far worse than leaving it alone."

Madelyn's shivering had started some chain reaction in her body, a rogue force taking over her senses before she could tamp it down. While she stared into Georgie's eyes, tears built in her own.

Don't make a scene about a baby deer, Mads.

But Georgie's stubbornness, her rejection of the idea took on a larger meaning in Madelyn's mind. It wasn't a rebuttal of the proposal to rescue the fawn, but instead a repudiation of Madelyn herself. Of vulnerability and openness. Madelyn blinked aggressively, trying to stop the tears before they could start flowing.

"Seems sad is all," she said, managing to sound like her throat wasn't constricting with emotion. She was impressed with herself. Concealing negative feelings wasn't her forte.

Georgie knew Madelyn too well to skim over the obvious way she was shutting down and bailing out of the conversation. It was normal for Georgie to be taciturn, not Madelyn. In the conversation's pause, Madelyn tried her best to smile at Georgie, to show her that she wasn't shaken by the prospect of leaving a baby deer alone in a snowstorm, but it failed.

Georgie saw what Madelyn was trying to hide, and she wavered.

"We can't bring the fawn with us, Mads. I'm sorry." Georgie's voice was softer, speaking gently to Madelyn as if Madelyn were also a shivering baby animal. Georgie's mittened hand reached out and patted Madelyn's arm. Madelyn watched it happen like it was in slow motion, a gesture that was welcome but alien all the same.

"Ok," said Madelyn. Her scarf muffled her voice, but the sentiment was clear. The two of them turned back to the trail and waded through the churned-up snow to the cabin. Their return journey was even more quiet than the snowshoe out to the clearing. Flakes still fell around them, tumbling from branches when the wind blew just right, and Madelyn took pleasure in seeing her breath puff into the chilled air.

She hoped the fawn wouldn't succumb to the cold. Maybe its mother was waiting in the trees outside the clearing, ready to return to its baby when the human intruders left. Madelyn had to think that was true, because the alternative depressed her too much. The mental picture of those huge, softly liquid brown eyes staring at her was etched in her mind.

Back at the cabin, stripped of their snowshoes and bulky winter gear, Madelyn's angst reared its head again. She saw the casual lines of Georgie's outfit and wished she'd been more assertive about what she wanted. Not just with the deer—with everything. Her plan had been to tell Georgie about her feelings over a nice glass of wine at dinner, or maybe curled up with blankets by the fire while they drank hot chocolate.

The storm was changing all her plans.

Before Madelyn could reconsider her brashness, before

she could even think about what it would mean coming on the heels of a strangely emotional disagreement about a fawn, she spoke. Georgie's back was turned as she brushed snow from the front of her jeans.

"I'm in love with you," Madelyn said. The words she'd rehearsed in front of the bathroom mirror for months now. The recipient, as always, Georgie, short hair tousled from exertion in the outdoors, shoulders rugged and completely impossible to read. But Madelyn hadn't thought about the way her stomach would liquefy in response to her confession.

She hadn't pictured—at least not accurately—how her heart would pound violently, sickeningly in her chest. Each reverberation shook her ribcage to the point where she could very well have been convinced she was having a heart attack. Logic dissuaded her of that notion, but this was a time of emotion prevailing.

At least for Madelyn.

She willed Georgie to turn. To respond.

Say anything, anything at all. It would be better than silence.

Georgie continued to wipe her hands over the front of her jeans, continued to stay facing away from Madelyn. If the signs in her own body hadn't reminded her, viscerally, that she'd just said the words she had needed to for oh so long, Madelyn could have thought that this was just another moment. Another part of a cabin trip, like the trips they'd had for years prior.

There had been no perceptible reaction on Georgie's part.

"Georgie?" said Madelyn. She couldn't bear the silence. It was already a far different response from the one she'd hoped would happen: that Georgie would smile and burst into some form of shy but happy grin, free to respond in kind with love.

Madelyn had been delusional.

She saw that now.

Because Georgie whirled around, eyes blazing with dark fury, and stared her down. The impression was one of a caged animal forced to confront its attacker. Desperation and rage sang in a chorus that rang out from Georgie's tensed body.

"What?"

"I said I'm in love with you," Madelyn said, her voice quieter now. She shook, literally shook as if she were freezing, but she knew it was nerves. The outpouring of relief in her body from having finally done the thing, from speaking when silence was easier, from breaking a seal that had invisibly divided her from her true self.

"And what the hell makes you think that's ok?" whispered Georgie. The quiet of her voice was in no way able to obscure the hurt in every syllable. While she might appear to be angry, Madelyn could sense myriad other emotions swimming beneath the surface.

"Can we sit down to talk about this?" asked Madelyn, gesturing to the couch in the living area. They were still standing in the cramped back door hallway, snow from their boots melting into puddles flecked with mud and pine needles. Madelyn had stepped in one of the wet spots without meaning to and now her sock stuck damply to her heel.

"Why?" asked Georgie. "Feeling trapped? Like, oh, I don't know, alone in a cabin in a fucking snowstorm with someone?"

"Woah, hey. I didn't plan that there'd be a snowstorm."

"You had a plan, though? Like you actually sat there and

thought 'what a great idea, I'll tell Georgie I'm in love with her on this trip'?"

Madelyn could have been mistaken, but she thought she saw tears in Georgie's eyes. It had been a long time since she'd seen Georgie emotional like that, and the discomfort she felt in knowing she was the cause overshadowed all other feelings.

"I'm sorry, we don't have to go anywhere."

"That's the point, Madelyn! We *can't* go anywhere right now. You let me come up here for a trip—hell, let me surprise you with an early arrival—and thought it was a great idea to blindside me with this...this..."

"Confession."

"Ambush."

The two words commingled in the air, leaving a heavy, painful silence as they each processed the meaning of the other's statement. Tension crackled and Madelyn wished she'd been smart enough to hold off. Something about that fawn, though, had triggered a need to start the process. Whether she found out Georgie hated her for saying it or whether she thought there could be a future where they were together, Madelyn had to act.

"I didn't mean for you to feel ambushed," said Madelyn at the same time as Georgie paced through the hallway and out into the main living area. She'd been cooped up in the small space with Madelyn long enough, apparently. Georgie kept moving, her socked feet taking her from the now-empty fireplace over to the kitchen island and back, over and over.

"I'm guessing you also didn't think about whether it could come across that way, though, hey?"

When Georgie asked the question of Madelyn, she shot her a glance with fiery eyes, the dark brown of her irises vivid with emotion. It was clear from Georgie's posture that a multitude of feelings were fighting inside of her; she paced with clenched fists and slouched even more than usual. Madelyn had followed her to the living room and sat nervously on the couch.

This wasn't the scene she'd hoped to see.

"I'm sorry, Georgie. I didn't think enough about you in this. I mean, obviously I was thinking about you. And my feelings for you. I needed to get it out there, get my feelings off my chest before I swallowed them forever. Just in case. But I didn't consider how much it might upset you to hear me say that."

Georgie laughed, a brittle barking sound that startled Madelyn out of her rambling.

"What?" asked Madelyn.

Georgie had reached the island again and swung around to return to the fireplace. The light streaming in the window had the cool tone of the snow itself, which fluttered about madly like nothing was happening inside this cabin that nature hadn't seen before. Madelyn ached to calm Georgie's nerves by leaving her alone but knew that their isolation kept her there.

"You can be so dramatic, Madelyn," answered Georgie. "I'm not suggesting you 'swallow' your feelings forever, just that you think for a few minutes about how your actions might affect others before you plunge me into something like this. I mean, couldn't you have called me? You didn't visit Edmonton once in this past year. Wouldn't it have been better to tell me on my home turf?"

Queasiness descended from the nape of Madelyn's neck down her throat and to her belly. The silence became unbearable, broken only by a gust of wind tossing snowflakes against the large glass window for a second, skittering away moments later. Georgie was right, of course. She so often was.

"I was scared," Madelyn said, her voice shaky. She cursed herself again for having such thin barriers between her composure and emotional meltdowns. It was something she'd always admired about Georgie: that she could be catastrophically upset but avoid bursting into tears.

"And I was lonely as fuck, Madelyn."

A small, split-second hint of vulnerability escaped from Georgie, and Madelyn grabbed hold of it with desperation. This was her road back in, the sign she needed to keep going and not give up. Georgie raged not because she hated Madelyn, nor because she felt nothing for her. There were always going to be difficult conversations following this confession. Always.

"I know. I just—the way we left things, when you left. It made it seem like you didn't want me to come visit. Or at least that it should have been on your terms. Your invitation. Was I supposed to ignore that? Push through the buffer you set up and disregard anything you'd said when you left?"

"I don't know," snapped Georgie, but Madelyn had seen the opportunity. Already the pacing had softened to a confused stroll, and Georgie faltered near the couches. She turned to face Madelyn and then leaned her arms onto the back of the couch across from Madelyn's. "Probably not."

"Listen. You have every right to be upset with me. I can acknowledge that I did *not* approach this the right way. I mean, I one hundred percent didn't intend to blurt out my true feelings in the back hallway of some cabin we're snowed into. That's not how I pictured this happening. And not just because of how I pictured it, but because of what you deserve. Candlelight, romance, all that corny jazz. You're special, Georgie. As a person, and to me."

Georgie's expression could have been described just then as a glower. She hunched over the couch staring at Madelyn with a furrowed brow and pursed lips. In her eyes, there was a peculiar light that struck a strange balance between fury and affection. But she softened, and she walked around to sit down on the couch.

"So what'd you picture happening? You'd woo me with some steak and then spell 'I love you' with chocolate sauce on ice cream?"

Madelyn still heard venom in Georgie's words, but the other woman's eyes had warmed, her posture shifted. Already, the ice between them had softened slightly. She wished she hadn't gone about things all wrong, but if they were truly meant to be together—a fact Madelyn had discovered in Georgie's absence and now held dearly to be one of the defining features of her life—they would find a way.

You could always find a way to improve things.

"Hardly," said Madelyn with a smile. "I had a plan, but you surprised me showing up here early."

"That was the intention. A surprise. Didn't know I'd be surprising your love confession plans, though."

"No, I know," Madelyn sighed. "Realistically, it's not so much that you were early as that I was late. I should have told you how I felt months ago, when I first figured it out for myself. Rather than sitting on it and waiting for the perfect moment to orchestrate something that would dazzle you."

"Well," said Georgie. She stretched her wrists and looked around the cabin with a half-smile. "We've always known you were a late bloomer, right?"

Madelyn welcomed the thaw happening in Georgie already, even though Madelyn knew she didn't deserve it.

Georgie's happiness would always have an effect on Madelyn.

"Hey now. I don't know if it's that I was a late bloomer, or that you were always the early bird."

The two women smiled, surprising themselves and each other by the way that fondness could creep back into the conversation, despite everything. Or maybe because of everything that had transpired between them. Georgie and Madelyn's interactions never started from the ground floor; they always built on so much shared history that no one emotion could rule completely.

Gusting wind brought down a puff of snow from the cabin roof, landing in the drift near the window with a soft thump.

"Guess I like to get a head start on," said Georgie. And though Madelyn was still so tense she was certain she could have jumped a full foot off the couch had she been startled by a tap on the shoulder, she was able to see how blurting the words out hadn't been as cataclysmic as she thought. At least for now.

7

AGE 12

They were in Georgie's bedroom when she knew she had to say it. Weeks had gone by since she'd finally admitted to herself that she was gay. Years spent wishing she could rescue Princess Leia suddenly sharpened to clarity about so much more. Lesbian, strange word though it was, fit her now.

She just hadn't told anyone else yet.

Madelyn and Georgie spent every day after school together, huddled in blankets on the couch watching The Simpsons and reruns of Degrassi, making jokes about which kids in their class would like the story lines they liked.

It was into this seemingly iron-clad bond that Georgie had to lob her new identity. She wanted to tell Madelyn and then have the option to run away. Because the truth was, she didn't know of anyone who was a lesbian in real life. Everyone knew Ellen DeGeneres was one, but in Calgary?

At their school?

Georgie would be alone.

She hoped that Madelyn wouldn't be mad at her. Friends were supposed to be there for you no matter what, but there were so many things Georgie felt she was supposed to be that she couldn't: boy crazy, girly, polite, organized. The words 'supposed to' had begun to lose meaning for her. She didn't fit into boxes.

When Madelyn and Georgie walked to Georgie's house after school that day, Georgie played with a frayed thread on her t-shirt mindlessly. She watched as Madelyn thanked Caroline for the snacks she made, and she observed the careful snubbing Portia and Ariel gave to them, as always. The older girls were using the television, so Madelyn and Georgie had to retreat to Georgie's room.

Fine by her. Privacy for a conversation she worried would end everything. If Madelyn thought she was gross and didn't want to be friends anymore, Georgie wasn't sure what she would tell her mother. She wasn't ready for that conversation. Madelyn would be the first person she told, for better or worse.

"Did you see Lost this week?" she asked Madelyn, though she suspected the answer already. Madelyn's mother couldn't afford cable even though her new job paid much better than before, so Madelyn only saw Lost if she happened to be over at Georgie's house on Wednesday nights.

Madelyn shook her head and fiddled with the Game Boy Advance Georgie had left on the floor.

"It was really good."

"Ok," said Madelyn, barely paying attention to Georgie's anxious small talk. "Maybe I'll see it later on a rerun."

"Who's your favorite character? Mine's Kate."

Georgie could hear how her voice was strained, rushed. Madelyn made a puzzled face as if she could sense that something was amiss with Georgie, but she wasn't sure what.

"I don't know. Charlie?"

"I think Kate's really pretty."

Georgie's heart fluttered when she said Kate's name, partially from the crush she had on the character and partially from admitting it out loud. She hoped Madelyn could intuit what she meant and that the conversation could end there.

"I guess so," said Madelyn. "When she's not all muddy."

Georgie wanted to retort that the mud was part of what made Kate so attractive: she was a rough and tumble girl, like Georgie, and looked her best when she was in the midst of something tense. Georgie liked Kate dirty; merely thinking about a recent scene made her blush.

"I have a crush on Kate," Georgie said, her voice a little too loud for the conversation because of nerves.

Whether Madelyn was immediately repulsed or not, she didn't show it. A small smile appeared on her face and she looked Georgie in the eye.

"Ooo, Georgie's got a crush!"

"No, I'm serious. I really like Kate. Because..."

Georgie took a deep breath.

"Because I'm a lesbian."

"Oh. Ok," said Madelyn.

The simplicity of her words made Georgie's stomach quiver. It couldn't be that easy.

Could it?

"I have a crush on Charlie," said Madelyn, leaning forwards with the same conspiratorial tone as Georgie. The way she bit her lip made Georgie think, momentarily, that

Madelyn was joking. But then Madelyn flushed pink and giggled. A blush was hard to fake.

So this was the moment. She'd told someone. Not just anyone: her best friend, Madelyn. And, truth be told, it had gone far better than Georgie had thought it would.

"If Charlie was a girl would you like him? Or still Kate?" said Madelyn. The curiosity in her eyes was pure, and Georgie's veins coursed with relief. There was a pounding sound in her head that could have been her heartbeat, relentless and vivid. Beneath her sweater, Georgie's back prickled with sweat.

"I don't know," she said. "I hadn't thought about that. What do you think?"

"What do I think you'd think?" asked Madelyn, laughing.

"No, I mean, yes. I don't know. I'm just talking nonsense."

The reality was that confessing her secret to Madelyn had taken up most of Georgie's brain power. All that seemed to be left was a humming sensation between her ears and the intense physical relief still flooding her body. Nothing cognitive was happening in a meaningful way.

"Do you wish you were Jack or Sawyer?" Madelyn said, tilting her head to the side while she waited for Georgie's response.

"Neither?"

"But they like Kate. They're fighting over her, so you'd be one of them if you were on the island."

"I don't know," said Georgie. Her chest still fought her when she tried to speak, still tightened like it was trying to keep her from spilling any more secrets out into the open. It seemed too good to be true for Madelyn to accept her without anger. Everyone who had said the word lesbian before around Georgie hadn't meant it to be a positive thing.

"I just want to be me, but with Kate. Like I'm a girl, and she's a girl. My girlfriend, you know?"

"So you'd just be you. On the island."

"Yeah, exactly." She smiled at Madelyn.

Would her friend still be her friend after this?

She hadn't thought it could be possible to maintain the same connection. It had eaten at her insides for weeks as she thought about it. She'd been sure Madelyn would push her away. And then Madelyn would tell someone because she was so creeped out and soon everyone would know, and then Georgie wouldn't have friends at all.

"Isn't she kind of old for you?" Madelyn said, raising her eyebrows. She laughed at her own joke.

"I mean, yeah. Ok. She's a full grown-up, but adults get married to people who aren't the same age all the time. Like Hugh Hefner."

"Who's Hugh Hefner?"

If Georgie had thought telling her friend about being gay was a difficult conversation, she certainly hadn't considered how to explain Playboy magazine. That was an accidental discovery from her father's study that she knew she wasn't supposed to have heard of, let alone seen. Plus, the women in the magazine always looked so unhappy and mean.

Georgie wanted to have a magazine with the boobs and everything, but where the women smiled at you and seemed to be having a good time. That was part of what she liked about Kate on Lost: her smile. Her mind wandered for a few seconds while she fell back into thinking about Kate and her toothy grin.

"Georgie?" asked Madelyn.

"He makes magazines with naked women in them. And

he's married or dated like a billion women. All younger than him, some by a lot."

"At once?!" yelped Madelyn. She'd been shocked by so much of that sentence, she clearly didn't know where to start. It took Georgie a moment to decipher what Madelyn was reacting to.

"No, I don't think so. Like break-ups and divorces and stuff."

"How do you know about him?"

There was another pause while Georgie considered how much she should tell. Implicating her father in the conversation was one thing, but admitting that she'd found the magazines and looked at them too was another. Madelyn had accepted her confession, yes, but would she be ok with this?

Georgie didn't want to push her luck. Madelyn probably wouldn't want to know about Georgie looking at pictures like that. She'd stuff her ears and yelp or something.

"Do you promise not to hate me?"

The intensity of Madelyn's response surprised Georgie. "I couldn't hate you, not ever. We're best friends."

The tightness in Georgie's chest returned, but happier this time. She felt a swelling of gratitude, for being able to live this life where she had a friend like Madelyn. For the way that Madelyn smiled at her, exactly the way Madelyn had smiled at Georgie for years now.

She truly felt like nothing had changed, except that now Georgie felt a thousand times better about being a lesbian. If Madelyn could still be her friend, maybe everything would turn out ok after all. How would a little conversation about naked pictures change things?

"We are best friends, aren't we?" said Georgie, smiling. "So you can't tell anyone else. I was looking for a book I'd been reading that my mom cleaned up, except she put it in my dad's office. I'm not really supposed to go in there, cause he hates when we get it messy. Anyway, I was going through piles and looking at all the books but not finding anything. Only, there was a pile of papers that had a board underneath it in the drawer, and the board was kind of loose. If you took the board away, there were magazines underneath. Playboy magazines. They're super dirty."

"Dirty like how?"

It was clear that Madelyn's interest had gone from the purity of a celebrity crush to a more transgressive curiosity. Georgie had felt the same thing when she saw the cover of that first Playboy. It had been like having a dream where Kate was kissing her, only Georgie was still awake, and everything tingled.

"The girls were naked. And some of them were touching themselves or doing things to look sexy. It was weird."

Georgie screwed up her nose partly in show—though she'd told Madelyn about her sexuality she wasn't sure she was ready to share how the Playboys had made her feel. What if that was where the line had been drawn, and once they crossed it Madelyn would abandon her?

Madelyn surprised Georgie, though, and spoke with bright eyes. "Are they still there?"

"What?"

"The magazines. Downstairs?"

Discomfort washed over Georgie, her scalp crawling with a chill of anxiety. But excitement rose up, too, to combat the feeling. She was torn between lies and truth.

"Yeah, I hid them back in the drawer after I saw. Sometimes I go look when no one's around."

That was as much as she wanted to confess. Other, more shameful thoughts of what she did after she looked weren't for sharing. Madelyn might have been understanding so far, but Georgie was loath to push her luck to the edge. Sweaty, exciting experiences were still just for Georgie and her imagination to enjoy.

"Can we go see them now?" said Madelyn, her forehead creased with an earnest expression that made Georgie long to do whatever Madelyn wanted. Her hair was parted exactly at the center of her head and it emphasized the way Madelyn had of raising her eyebrows when she asked a meaningful question.

Georgie knew she shouldn't. All of her previous trips to the study had been when her father was working late and her mother and sisters were driving to ballet lessons or picking up groceries. A few had been when the family was outside enjoying the patio later at night or shoveling snow, but never had Georgie opened that drawer with other members of the family still in the house.

Georgie wasn't sure what Madelyn wanted out of the venture, nor was she certain that she could trust that their friendship would remain unchanged, even though she so desperately wanted it to. And yet, here was a chance to grow closer. To reveal a hidden part of her life, maybe to be seen as more valid.

And yet.

While Madelyn's question hung in the air, Georgie bit her lip and thought. Snapshots of the fleshy images she'd seen already brewed in the back of her mind, heating her thoughts to a dangerous place. Even if it was a terrible idea, Georgie wanted to see a Playboy right now.

She wanted to open those glossy pages and see a woman, naked, breasts exposed invitingly so that Georgie's heart hammered and her body rushed with longing.

A glimpse of parts she still wouldn't say out loud yet.

Feverish tension building between her legs, demanding her attention.

Even if Madelyn saw the magazine and ran from the house screaming, Georgie now thought she could handle it.

In part because she wasn't thinking rationally at all anymore.

"Yeah, if we're quiet, we can go right now," whispered Georgie. She held a finger before her lips and hunched her shoulders, padding along the carpet in her bedroom to the door. Madelyn followed her, breathing through her mouth so audibly Georgie would have normally cancelled the mission.

But Georgie saw this point in time as a narrow window of opportunity. Her mother was baking seasonal cookies and her sisters were in the basement watching a movie. Georgie's father never came home this early. And besides, it wasn't every day that your best friend heard that you were a lesbian and then wanted to see naked women with you.

Georgie almost couldn't believe her luck.

She willed her mother to keep baking, her sisters to sit passively absorbing their movie. Madelyn walked softly behind her, and with each step Georgie's skin tingled a little more. They were downstairs within a minute, and Georgie held up a hand to indicate a pause near the landing.

She heard the stand mixer working in the kitchen and motioned for Madelyn to follow her while she rounded the corner to the hall. A few more steps, and then they were in the study. Georgie flicked on the overhead light and breathed deeply for the first time in what seemed like forever. Madelyn was smiling next to her, her hands visibly shaking from the adrenaline.

"They're just in here," whispered Georgie. She'd crossed the thick hunter green rug to the desk, which was immaculately clean as always, and opened the bottom right-hand drawer. A stack of innocuous papers in firm-branded folders were inside, which she took out and put on the desk.

Beneath the papers, she found the false bottom of the drawer easily. Once you knew it was there, the seam was obvious. Georgie's slim fingers hooked around the board quickly and she lifted it while Madelyn watched, eyes huge and rapt.

"I can't believe we're doing this," Madelyn said with a nervous giggle.

Georgie smiled in a way she hoped appeared reassuring, and she picked up a shiny copy of Playboy. It was one she hadn't seen before, so she knew that her father replenished the supply occasionally.

Excitement built a ramp in her stomach and began to race upwards.

Madelyn stepped closer to look over Georgie's shoulder while she leafed through the pages. Madelyn gasped when they reached the centerfold.

"Wow," whispered Madelyn. "I hope I get big boobs someday, too."

Georgie just smiled, not wanting to say that she was less keen on growing her own breasts to that size so much as finding someone with similar proportions she could touch. Madelyn's reaction felt so different from hers.

"Do you think—" Madelyn began to speak, but her voice cut short when the door opened in front of them and Georgie's mother's face poked in.

"Girls? What are you doing in here?"

One of Georgie's most poignant regrets in the years that followed was that she hadn't positioned the stack of accounting papers as a barrier to someone who entered the office after them. As it played out in her mind, she and

Madelyn could have hidden the dirty magazine behind that paper wall so that her mother never knew what was going on.

In real life, of course, things went much differently. Caroline's eyes dropped from the two girls' faces to the sleekly gorgeous woman on the cover of the magazine, and it was less than a second after asking her question that she gasped and yelled for them to get out of there.

8

PRESENT DAY

"You knew you were a lesbian so early on, Georgie. I'd been jealous of your certainty for a long time. Recently, though, I've wondered if you sometimes choose to see things more black and white because you like being definite. Or pretending to be, if you have to."

Georgie made a face and stared Madelyn down. "What does that mean?"

They were still across from one another on the couches, still locked in a difficult conversation. The snow fell faster now, determined to blanket the countryside in so much of itself that the landscape would be unrecognizable.

"Do you really, completely and totally think we have zero chance of being together? If you knew that, deep down in your bones, and had absolutely no doubts about it... it would be easier for me to accept your saying no. But I can't buy it, at least not yet. Isn't there some small part of you that sees a chance for us?"

Madelyn spoke with more confidence than she had. It was excruciating to see the anger and disdain on Georgie's intelligent features. Even as the light dimmed outside, bringing the dark December evening ever closer, Madelyn couldn't fight the spark inside her. Whether it was hope or something less admirable, she couldn't tell.

All she knew was that she wanted Georgie to be in her life, more than she'd wanted anything else in this world.

"Since when is a chance worth throwing away everything?" Georgie said, having deliberated silently for a minute after Madelyn spoke.

"So there is one? A chance?"

A heavy sigh rushed out of Georgie. In the rapidly darkening afternoon light, she looked younger. Without the experience of seeing one another regularly, Madelyn found she'd been picturing a version of Georgie where she'd aged and matured much differently. Georgie still carried herself with a sort of impish swagger, but the curve of her cheeks reminded Madelyn of when Georgie was just a kid.

Sometimes Madelyn felt she was still a child, too. Lost in the murky depths of trying to grow up and figure herself out. How it was possible to reach 25 and still assume you were 16 when people asked your age, she didn't know. Maybe you never felt grown up. Maybe it was all a lie that everyone pretended was real, so they didn't feel as scared by the world.

"The hell am I supposed to say to that, Mads? The issue isn’t whether there’s some microscopic chance. It seems like you’ve got a whole other version of me playing out like a movie in your head."

"Translation, I should move on?"

Georgie rolled her eyes in frustration. "That's a perfect example of what I mean. You're so good at taking what I say as this horrible, cruel thing. I never said it with that... tone. You're the one making me sound mean."

Madelyn struggled to reconcile her rushing feelings with the retreat Georgie was making. Georgie's elbows were on her knees, and she'd run her hands through her hair angrily while talking. It left a shaggy trail of cowlicks behind and tenderness leapt into Madelyn's chest, unbidden.

Georgie had that way about her of making Madelyn care. Especially when she wanted to do anything but get entangled in another person's emotions.

"Sorry if my feelings are inconvenient to you, Georgie," Madelyn said. She regretted the childishness of her statement seconds later. "I shouldn't have said that. What I meant was, I hoped you'd feel differently. That maybe there was a spark."

This time, it was Georgie's turn to falter. She drew her legs up underneath her and looked as if she were about to speak a few times before she actually got words out.

"I've started dating. In Edmonton."

"Oh."

Panic and dread made a terrible combination, seeping into every fiber of Madelyn's body until it was immobilized. It would be just her luck to realize she loved Georgie right after Georgie moved to Edmonton, only to lose her to another woman with better timing.

Did she have a girlfriend?

Madelyn didn't have the courage to ask.

"How's it going?" she said, instead.

The casual shrug with which Georgie responded would have been enough to plunge Madelyn into depression if she hadn't already taken down all the walls surrounding her heart for this conversation. No barriers remained, so instead the way Georgie seemed to want things to stay irreverent merely stung Madelyn. Like wasps on a hot summer night.

"Anyone special?" Madelyn asked, and then she realized

she'd bitten her lip. The coppery tang of blood mixed with her regrets and it became too much, all at once. "Actually, don't answer that."

Georgie faltered, her eyes searching Madelyn's face for insight.

"Are you ok?" said Georgie, but at the same time, Madelyn stood abruptly.

"I should go to bed," she said.

Georgie laughed until she realized Madelyn was serious. "But it's 3:00."

Madelyn waved her hand vaguely and started walking to the stairs. "A nap, then. I need to sleep. Right now."

Her body had almost shut down. Too much input, too much feeling, had worn her down to bone-dry exhaustion. She had sudden sympathy for her computer's restless whirring after a long evening of homework, when its fan couldn't keep up with the processor despite desperately trying to cool the machine.

"All right," Georgie said. She watched Madelyn step up the staircase one tread at a time with wary concern. If she had more questions, she didn't ask them then.

Madelyn was grateful when she put her head on the pillow and sleep followed quickly; she'd been afraid of the afternoon's conversation playing over and over in her head. Sometimes she got stuck on a moment like that and couldn't help but relive it, trying to find a way to make it go how she'd wanted. Today, though, her body collapsed readily.

Sleep was a welcome oblivion.

The lightest rap on the door woke Madelyn. Her open

mouth had drooled a small puddle next to the pillow, and she grunted in confusion when the noise came again.

"Madelyn?"

The voice belonged to someone familiar. Madelyn's sleep-addled brain struggled to place it.

"What time is it?" she asked, noticing the pitch-black surroundings. She was at the cabin in the mountains.

With Georgie.

Remembering the conversation they'd had earlier, Madelyn wished she could return to sleep. But Georgie had opened the door a crack and poked her head in.

"Hey. Sorry to wake you. There's food downstairs if you want a meal. But... I should let you know the power's out."

The whirring of Madelyn's mind sped up tenfold and she bolted upright.

"What?"

"It's kept on snowing outside. Must have knocked a power line down somewhere. The stove's gas, so I could make some pasta, but the lights are out, and the baseboard heaters don't work anymore."

"Shit."

Silence allowed Madelyn to listen for the storm. Wind howled outside, casting flakes against the window in chaotic smatterings. It sounded rough out there. Luckily, the weather eclipsed her hurt feelings, because Madelyn was also hungry.

"There any pasta left?" she said, not quite ready to meet Georgie's eye. Thankfully, it was dark enough that she thought Georgie might not notice.

"Tons."

With a stretch, Madelyn stood up and followed Georgie down to the kitchen. Where she'd expected darkness, there was a fire crackling in the hearth. Though it was more dimly lit than the cabin would have been with electricity, the flickering brightened the space considerably.

"Good job on that fire, G."

"Thanks," said Georgie. She stared into the fire when they reached the bottom of the stairs, causing shadows to cast about her face in dancing motions. Madelyn could have gazed at Georgie's implacable expression for ages, but her stomach had other plans. While they stood there for a moment, a growl escaped her belly.

Madelyn laughed. "Sorry, I guess my strategy of bailing from a difficult conversation mid-day has angered my stomach."

Georgie didn't respond, just smiled weakly. Madelyn wished she knew what Georgie was thinking. But she didn't press her. She suspected her nap had also angered Georgie. It had been insensitive.

"And it's probably infuriated the electricity gods, too, by the look of it," Madelyn said. Even if Georgie was mad at her, Georgie was too kind a person not to offer a meal to Madelyn. And now, survival had to transcend their own personal drama. Being stranded in the woods with no power was dangerous.

A steaming bowl of fusilli later, Madelyn dabbed red sauce from her mouth with a napkin and went to the couches to join Georgie. Though the fire wasn’t as high as when she came downstairs, white-hot coals shimmered at the bottom of the hearth, emitting more warmth than the licking flames had earlier.

Madelyn sat on the couch across from Georgie and watched as a log capsized, tumbling into the coals with a fizz of sparks.

"You made a great fire," she said to Georgie. With her belly full of pasta and a nap under her belt, the heart-wrenching talk of the afternoon felt miles away. They still had time to work through things. No matter what they wanted to do, the weather had them stuck.

Georgie stared into the fire, her face unreadable. She was curled up beneath a throw blanket and the only thing moving about her was a foot that poked out from the side of the throw, tapping restlessly. She may not have heard Madelyn's comment.

"It's nothing serious," said Georgie. Though she didn't turn to face Madelyn, the words sounded heavy with emotion.

"Oh, I don't know. Might not seem like it now, but if we have no heat, I'm definitely glad you know how to start and tend a fire. My post-apocalyptic knowledge is more like 'Ask Georgie for help' and 'Die if zombies find me'."

Madelyn found herself smiling just from being near Georgie. She knew she sounded silly—that was often the case when she spent time with her best friend. Georgie was so withdrawn sometimes, so serious. It made Madelyn feel like a glass of champagne that couldn't stop bubbling.

"No. I mean that no one I've been on a date with is serious. Or that no dates have been serious. Whatever, you get the point."

Pop. Fizz. The champagne shouldn't have been celebrating as much as it was, but Madelyn wasn't so altruistic as to wish her love interest off the market. She wanted Georgie to be happy, yes, but ideally that happiness could be found with her.

"I do," she said. "Thanks for telling me. Can I ask—"

But Madelyn wasn't able to finish her question because Georgie stood up abruptly. The glimpse of vulnerability she'd allowed Madelyn apparently couldn't be sustained. "Fire's not enough to keep this place warm all night. The pipes might freeze up, so we should run the taps just in case."

"Ok. Good idea." Madelyn followed Georgie to the main floor bathroom, where she cranked the tub to the slowest trickle possible while Georgie let the sink tap flow. In this proximity, it was hard not to notice the lean muscles that made up the lines of Georgie's body, the collarbone that ran across her shirt opening. Madelyn's nerves tingled while her eyes betrayed her.

"I like your shirt," she said, hoping a compliment would explain why she'd been staring. Georgie shrugged and grinned bashfully, holding out the sides of the button-up.

"This old thing? I've had it for years."

"I know. It looks good on you," Madelyn said. She walked out of the bathroom to fill the kitchen sink, hoping she'd finish blushing before Georgie saw her face.

Why couldn't she just keep things under wraps for a better time?

It wasn't like a snowstorm was the right moment to shower a friend in compliments. It had hardly been opportune for her to confess her feelings, either. Madelyn was just plain bad at the whole thing. She deserved the frustrations Georgie had been expressing, and then some.

They continued the task upstairs in each of the bathrooms and then settled back in near the fire. The wind outside provided a constant background noise, blasting the large glass panes in the front of the cabin with periodic gusts of snow.

For all the noise coming from nature, the inside of the building was silent. Without the hum of the fridge or lights coming from appliances, it was eerily calm. All that pierced the weather-driven howl was the fire, cheery in its persistence. Madelyn felt nervous for the first time that they'd overstay their time booked here.

"When do you think we'll be able to shovel out our cars and drive home?"

"Depends on when it stops snowing this much. And when they get a plow out here."

"Yikes," said Madelyn. "I think I need a drink. Wait. Should I not open the fridge to let the cold out?"

Georgie laughed, shaking her head at Madelyn. Her question had been well-intentioned but obviously amused Georgie. "The whole world's our fridge now, Mads."

"Riiiight," Madelyn said, smiling weakly. "Ok, now I really need a drink. That's embarrassing. You want one?"

Their tenuous rekindling of friendly words didn't seem threatened by the offer, but Madelyn found her palms damp with sweat all the same. If she offended Georgie by asking like everything hadn't been shattered into awkward pieces this afternoon, there was no escape.

They were stuck with each other.

But Georgie nodded, so Madelyn fetched them each a bottle of her favorite IPA. While they drank, they took the contents of the fridge out to a snowbank in the back, tossing the more solid items farther away from the door. Snow had already piled up enough by the entrance to make leaving the cabin difficult.

Once the task was finished, Georgie turned to Madelyn. Her posture shrunk inward, and her eyes barely met Madelyn's when she spoke.

"So listen. I wouldn't say this if I didn't think it was actually what we needed to do. I'm not trying to get you in bed with me. But it's going to get cold tonight, and we should stay down on the main level by the fire. Ideally, sharing a big sleeping bag or pile of blankets to conserve body heat. Again, I'm not trying to make things weird."

Madelyn smiled far too broadly for the situation, her desire to calm Georgie's nerves painfully apparent. "Not weird! I remember building quinzhees in Girl Guides when we learned about preserving warmth in winter."

"Good," Georgie smiled. Her eyes still skittered around Madelyn's nose and eyebrows when she did look at Madelyn directly. Never did she meet her gaze head on that night. "Let's check for two-person sleeping bags upstairs. I've got a flashlight in my duffel. You want to look through the closets downstairs and let me know if you find anything?"

It didn't take long, because the cabin was well stocked. Georgie hollered down to Madelyn with a report of success only a few minutes into their search. Madelyn wasn't sure whether she was relieved or terrified. Maybe a bit of both.

The two women sat on the couches, feeding logs into the fire while they sipped beer and chatted about the weather for as long as they could before it became clear that they both craved sleep. They hadn't dared venture into the topics of that afternoon's conversation, and neither was willing to be the first to crawl into bed.

The sleeping bag was draped over a camping mat Georgie had found in the closets upstairs, placed close enough to the fire to appreciate the warmth while it died down but not so close as to pose a fire hazard. It sat between them, beckoning, while they continued to avoid deep conversation.

Finally, Georgie yawned and went to leave her empty beer bottle near the sink.

"I'm beat and need to sleep." She slipped into the sleeping bag. Madelyn stared into the fireplace, wishing she'd been more cautious about expressing her feelings earlier that day.

No point in worrying over what's done.

The air downstairs was warmest close to the fireplace, so she ought to use the sleeping bag. Going upstairs to sleep alone, possibly to be chilled so badly she'd wake in the night full of regret, didn't make sense.

Madelyn joined Georgie in the sleeping bag, painfully aware of the warmth and proximity of Georgie's body. It wasn't until an hour had passed that she relaxed enough to fall asleep, wind still washing over the cabin in an off-beat rhythm of gusts.

9

Dawn lit the cabin grey and blue, casting long, eery shadows behind the furniture. Madelyn ached from sleeping on a simple mat on the floor, but she was cozy and warm inside the sleeping bag. The tip of her nose, however, had gone numb from the chill.

As Madelyn woke up, she noticed that Georgie's arm was wrapped around her torso. Georgie was spooning her gently, still breathing a deep, sleep-ridden rhythm. Though she knew she should lift Georgie's arm and shift away from her, Madelyn didn't want to. It felt too right.

She let herself lie there, comfortably wrapped in the woman she loved, until the sudden stiffening of Georgie's body signaled that she'd woken up. Apparently, she hadn't liked what she found.

"Shit," murmured Georgie, pulling away from Madelyn. In the absence of her arms around Madelyn's body, the cold crept in once more. Shared body heat had helped, whether Georgie's subconscious meant for her embrace to be heat-seeking or something more.

Georgie cleared her throat and unzipped her side of the

sleeping bag. She stood, shaking herself awake, and started to gather logs for a new fire while she shivered.

"Hey," said Madelyn. "Good morning."

"Oh, hi," Georgie said, whirling around. Her furtive slouch told Madelyn that Georgie was embarrassed to have come closer in the night, but Madelyn wasn't sure why. "I didn't know you were awake."

"The dawn woke me up."

As realization of what that meant grew in Georgie's mind, Madelyn watched a blush creep into Georgie's cheeks. The urge to save Georgie from awkwardness made Madelyn speak.

"And you were right, the sleeping bag and being next to each other helped me stay warm. I'm glad you were smart about that. I'd have done something stupid and regretted it."

"Ah, good."

"And if I do say so myself, you're an excellent big spoon."

Shit. That wasn't what was supposed to happen.

Madelyn had intended to provide Georgie with a safe out from the discomfort of waking up entwined together, had meant to pretend it wasn't a big deal. Except some devilish impulse inside Madelyn wanted to force things. There had to be a spark between them, otherwise what else could explain what happened?

If Madelyn's mind was grasping for proof that Georgie had any feelings for her, it apparently was going to rally all its strength to latch onto wisps of evidence. She steadied herself with a deep breath and watched Georgie's back while she lit tinder for the fire.

"Uh-huh," said Georgie. Either she wasn't paying attention, or she was buying time.

Madelyn approached the hearth, coming up behind Georgie with cautious steps, like she was a watchful deer that might bolt if a twig snapped. "Need a hand with anything?"

Georgie looked up, her eyes finally meeting Madelyn's purely by accident, and in those wide brown irises, Madelyn saw what she'd wanted to this whole year. It may have been the morning light, or the fact that Georgie was still waking up and therefore hadn't had time to draw the curtains closed on her feelings, but there was something there. A spark of the affection Madelyn had known.

"No, thanks," said Georgie, turning away to focus on the small flames curling around the tinder. The clench of Georgie's jaw as she wrestled with her demons accelerated Madelyn’s heartbeat.

"I'll make breakfast, then."

Ten minutes and a few eggs later, Madelyn brought a plate over to where Georgie sat on the couch. Georgie accepted the food, shoveling it into her mouth like she'd been starving for weeks.

"Looks like it's finally stopped snowing," Georgie said when she finished clearing the plate. She pointed out the front windows to the utterly still landscape beyond.

"Wow," breathed Madelyn. She had been so preoccupied with her feelings, with Georgie, that she hadn't appreciated their stunning surroundings. The huge panes of glass allowed a view of the heavily laden trees, the drifts that were piled up to the railing on the deck.

"It must have snowed two feet," said Georgie.

Madelyn couldn't think of a response. Perhaps none was necessary. The silence now sounded like a peculiar absence of wind. With the whole world around them blanketed so deeply, it seemed like noise had been outlawed and the rest of their lives would be lived in a perfect, wintry hush.

She was loath to break it.

Georgie spoke first, standing to clear the dishes to the sink. "We should get some more wood from the lean-to outside for today. The temperature's likely dropping as it clears up, and we've used most of the logs they had inside."

"Want help with that?" said Madelyn, meaning the dishes Georgie had stacked, but when Georgie smiled and nodded, she realized she'd agreed to help get firewood from outside. It didn't matter; what was important was they could spend time together. Maybe right the wrongs of Madelyn's ill-timed confession.

The water groaned through the pipes, but they were able to wash the dishes. Once the plates and cutlery were clean, Georgie suggested they fill a few pots with drinking water in case the pipes froze over.

"I don't know why I didn't think of that last night. Had other things on my mind, I guess."

"Like what?"

Georgie's face darkened at Madelyn's question. "You know what, Mads. Come on, let's get outside."

Each time Madelyn thought she was getting through to Georgie, she bounced up against another, deeper barrier. The girl was formidable for so many reasons, but in the year apart she seemed to have built even more defence mechanisms.

How had this never come up in their Skype dates?

Madelyn wondered if she'd been so focused on sorting out her own feelings that she'd neglected to consider Georgie's. It must have been hard to move to a new city and start over again, even harder for someone who'd always been quiet. Georgie had been so brave; Madelyn could appreciate that now.

When Madelyn opened the back door, she found their makeshift refrigeration area had been covered with snow overnight. A few beer bottle necks poked out of the lower areas on the drifts, but mostly the food and drink were obscured by snow.

They'd dressed warmly even though the lean-to was close, because once snow got into your socks or pant legs, it melted to a chilly dampness that would make things far more uncomfortable than they had to be. Madelyn waited for Georgie to finish putting on her scarf and then she smiled and leapt backwards into a drift, like she wanted to make a snow angel.

With a puff of fresh snowflakes, she landed to the left of the food.

"Come on in, the water's fine!" Madelyn said, grinning at Georgie. She waggled her arms and legs around and then righted herself. The snow came up to her hips and became much denser around the knee and lower. Wading to the lean-to would be difficult.

"How did you know you weren't going to hit food? Lucky. You always did love snow, didn't you?" said Georgie. She stepped into the drifts, shoving her mittened hands in her pockets at first until it became clear she'd need her arms out for balance while she moved. Madelyn fought a smile when Georgie wobbled and then righted herself. It was too endearing for words.

"Did I?" asked Madelyn, fighting forwards with a motion more like swimming than walking. The snow was formidable and did not care where she wanted to go. "I remember being a much bigger fan of summer than winter."

"What about all the snowball fights?" asked Georgie. Winter's chill added a soft pink to her nose, one that distracted Madelyn while she moved, ever so slowly, towards the stacked firewood.

"Those were fun. Too bad I was awful at throwing them.

I don't think a single snowball of mine actually landed on a target until at least... 2008? Maybe later."

"They didn't need to land, just intimidate. I was the sniper, and you were my cover fire."

Reminiscing with Georgie made Madelyn's chest ache with nostalgia for the time when they'd been so close, not just in the sense where they lived in the same city, but also for when they'd shared thoughts and feelings without a second's pause.

How had they gotten to now? Where Georgie had started trying to date and hadn't even spoken to Madelyn in weeks. Snow spilled into the space between Madelyn's boots and ankles, making her yelp at the sudden cold.

"What?"

"It's nothing," said Madelyn. She didn't want to be a bother. Except she took another step, misjudging the landscape because it was so deeply shrouded you couldn't gauge anything accurately, and she plunged a full foot deeper into a drift. When her boot landed, it slipped sideways and the painful twisting made her cry out. Ice crunched beneath her.

"Shit!"

"Mads?" said Georgie. She went as quickly as she could to Madelyn's side. Her speed was dampened by the drifts, but there was urgency to her movement. "Are you okay?"

Madelyn nodded, clenching her teeth as she tried to right herself. But putting weight on the foot sent throbbing pain up her leg, so she tried to steady herself on her good side. The snow came up almost to her chest in this spot, which from the ice crackling underneath her boots sounded like it was a frozen stream bed. That would explain the change in elevation.

"You go inside, and I'll get the firewood. Don't hurt yourself any worse than you have already."

Georgie's concerned brow furrow and the clipped brusqueness of her voice may have put off someone less acquainted with her personality. Beneath those prickly-seeming signals, Madelyn could sense how worried Georgie was about her. It warmed her better than the thermal underwear she'd brought for the trip.

"I'll try," said Madelyn. She didn't want to finish the thought, to express that she wasn't sure she could make it back to the door without help. It wasn't even that far away. She'd been wading slowly. But with the pain in her ankle as vivid as it was, Madelyn was worried about jolting or falling.

Still, she didn't want to ask Georgie for help. Too much guilt about spilling her feelings so messily still sat in Madelyn's shoulders, tightening muscles and pulling her inwards.

Madelyn took a breath, exhaling raggedly while she watched the air in front of her mouth steam visibly. She held her arms out to the side for balance and gingerly stepped backwards, trying to put only the slightest weight on the bad foot and then hop to the good immediately. Luckily, she'd forged a path from the door so the way back would be easier than if it were fresh snow.

Marginally easier.

Even the hint of weight on her bad ankle made Madelyn curse, breath shocked out of her like she'd been punched.

"Woah. Hey." Georgie fought the snow and came to Madelyn. "Put your arm around me."

She didn't have to ask twice. Madelyn melted onto Georgie for support and bit her lip to fight back tears. The pain seemed to lessen almost instantly, either because of the physical aid or the emotional relief. Their closeness to one another felt natural, like walking down a peaceful lane in the forest.

Except they were a handful of feet away from the back door of the cabin, surrounded by winter, not foliage. The wind had quieted down to a murmuring presence, and Madelyn's greatest concern was torn between wondering whether she'd broken her ankle and trying not to stare at Georgie's face when it was so close.

The two made their way slowly, pushing through the great drifts of snow in a careful churn. Georgie's strong shoulders lifted Madelyn upright, her firm hand on Madelyn's back a comfort at the same time as it was a hyper-focused presence in her mind. Madelyn wanted that hand to stay, to run up her back and into her hair, gently.

Though their progress was slow and, for Madelyn, painful, in the post-storm hush it felt as if a small blinking light had been re-lit. Madelyn still wished she hadn't blurted out her feelings earlier, but at least now she knew Georgie didn't hate her for it. She was still the same sturdy and caring woman she'd known all these years. Who Madelyn had fallen for, despite herself.

Inside, Georgie maneuvered Madelyn to a dining room chair and helped her sit down. She shut the door and brushed the dustings of snow off her various surfaces: boots, legs, waist. Madelyn tried to do the same but made a half-circle of rapidly melting snow around her seat.

"Oops," she said. "Guess I'll end up stepping in that when I get up again."

"No, I can help you out of it," Georgie said. She approached to help Madelyn with her winter gear, easing the boot off her injured foot with such steady, even caution that Madelyn found herself breathing like she was in a yoga class, deep and meditative. It ached, throbbing to a fever pitch when the boot rounded the widest part of her heel, but Madelyn counted in her head and managed not to swear.

She didn't realize she'd closed her eyes to make her way through the pain until she opened them and saw Georgie. Gone was the hurt she'd seen in Georgie's deep-set eyes and finely creased brow. It had been entirely replaced by concern for Madelyn. Basking in that care, she felt whole.

Georgie was so close, kneeling at Madelyn's lap, that Madelyn didn't dare breathe or disturb the moment. Whatever was transpiring between them had the fragility of a single snowflake, impossibly unique and delicate. Georgie's hands stayed on Madelyn's foot and calf, warm from the exertion outside.

Georgie opened her mouth to speak, words waiting for the right moment and then lingering a fraction of a second too long. Before Madelyn could do anything to make it easier for Georgie to say what she needed to, she felt hands slide up her legs. Sparks tingled their way along the path of Georgie's palms, still firm against Madelyn's body.

Once they reached the tops of Madelyn's thighs, Georgie's hands grasped the sides of the chair. She leaned in, so close that each muted freckle on her nose was visible. Madelyn shivered from nerves, not cold, and felt Georgie's lips meet her own. The kiss lasted a second, maybe two, and then Georgie stood.

Breaking the silence still felt impossible to Madelyn. She didn't dare speak and discover that Georgie regretted the moment that just happened. Because the tenderness between them was so precisely what Madelyn had craved for months now, she'd have pledged herself to silence for a lifetime if that was what it took to preserve things.

"I'm still mad at you," said Georgie. Her voice had a

husky quality to it, the kind that made it sound like she needed to clear her throat. She didn't. Just stood, head slightly tilted, while she gazed at Madelyn.

"If that's how you treat me when you're angry, I'll take it."

Madelyn wasn't sure if she were joking and flirtatious or utterly sincere. Maybe both.

"Don't get cocky," Georgie said, smirking. The twinkle in her eye as she said it almost took Madelyn's breath away. All the nights this year she'd spent wondering if Georgie could feel anything romantic for her now culminated in such simple flirtation that strangers wouldn't even remark upon it. To Madelyn, though, it was earth shaking.

"Not to worry. I've fucked up my ankle just so I can stay humble."

"Yeah, we should take a closer look at that," Georgie said, running her hand up the back of her neck, where she paused, awkwardly, and stood looking at Madelyn's foot. "Can you take off your sock?"

Madelyn wanted to ask Georgie to take it off for her, but she suspected overt flirtation would send her friend running outside in a panic. Firewood and snow drifts were likely better company than Madelyn's terrible jokes. She bent and peeled the sock off, gingerly moving it past her swelling ankle.

Georgie kneeled again, immediately sucking in a breath when she did so.

"Damnit. Now my pants are wet from the melting snow."

It was like she was trying to get Madelyn to say something dirty in response. Or was that just Madelyn's mind running wild, now that Georgie had kissed her?

That kiss had shifted everything.

Before, she'd been afraid that Georgie wanted nothing to do with her. Georgie's response to finding out Madelyn was in love with her hadn't exactly been happy. But now it seemed there was more lurking beneath the surface. Madelyn should have been frustrated to be stuck in a powerless cabin, her ankle sprained and painful. Instead, she was flushed with gratitude that the universe sent her this brief, bizarre moment in time.

It might just have been exactly what she needed to get close to Georgie.

10

"ARE YOU SURE YOU'RE COMFORTABLE?" ASKED GEORGIE. Madelyn wanted to laugh, having been swaddled in blankets on the couch, stuffed in between so many pillows she wasn't sure there was even room for a human body to join them. The side table Georgie had piled with snacks, water, and books sat within arm's reach, and the fire was crackling amiably.

"Yes. Now please go get more firewood. I'm growing accustomed to this level of luxury and if it dies down even a bit, I am sure I'll get a most frightful chill!" Madelyn grinned while she held the back of her hand to her forehead like a damsel in distress.

"At your service," said Georgie. She smiled just indulgently enough that Madelyn knew she hadn't pushed past that invisible boundary. The one where she'd flirt or joke too hard and Georgie might pull away indefinitely.

God, falling for your best friend was hard.

There'd been many times in the decades that they'd known each other when Madelyn had been thankful they'd met. In the months since Georgie had moved to Edmonton, Madelyn spent even more time thinking about her. It wasn't until she'd started dating women openly, trying to find the right person for the rest of her life, that she'd realized she was searching for something she'd already found.

And now she had her shot to convince Georgie that she deserved a real romantic chance.

Georgie stacked firewood from the lean-to in piles by the fire and then joined Madelyn in the living room. While Madelyn absentmindedly snacked on the popcorn twists Georgie had poured into a bowl for her, they sat enjoying the fire's heat.

“I said it before, but I’ll say it again: you make a good fire, Georgie. And thanks for helping me with my ankle. You're sure you don't think it's broken?"

A flash of uncertainty crossed Georgie's face, but she shook her head. "Not with the way you're able to move it right now. Just sprained, I'd say. But take the advice of a medical professional over mine when you're able to get out of here. I'm just a basic first aid kind of gal."

"And then some," said Madelyn. She smiled, hoping to catch Georgie's eye, but Georgie’s gaze was lost in the depths of the fire. "Now that we're cozy again... Would you mind telling me a bit about the dates you've been on? If you don't want to, I understand. But if you do, you know, I could help. Be your friend and confidant and all that kind of thing."

"Are you sure?"

Madelyn paused. She craved intimacy with Georgie more than anything, even if that disclosure would hurt. She'd rather know what kinds of women Georgie was seeing than not. Might as well. "Yes, of course! Just because I'm in love with you doesn't mean I don't want to be your friend."

Georgie frowned slightly and Madelyn backpedaled.

"I'm joking, Georgie. Joking! Too soon, though, hey?"

"You bet it's too soon." Georgie snorted with laughter and Madelyn felt the tightness in her belly shift.

"But I am serious. Any real prospects?"

"Huh. Not sure I'd say that," Georgie started. But she scratched her head and paused. "More just some fun."

“So like casual sex?"

"Are you really sure you want to talk about this? Couldn't it wait until we Skype next month or something?"

If Madelyn wasn't mistaken, Georgie was blushing. Georgie shifted in her seat, glancing at Madelyn without making eye contact.

"I'm hurt. Entertain me," said Madelyn. "It's the least you could do, since we don't even have Netflix."

"Ok then. I'll be Netflix."

"If your sex life in Edmonton was a Netflix show, what would its title be?"

Georgie groaned. "I don't know, 'Extremely Quiet and Incredibly Mediocre'?"

With a slap on her knee, Madelyn burst into laughter she didn't know she'd needed. "That's good. How about 'Awkward is the New Black'?"

"Or 'Blue is the Awkwardest Color'..."

"Good, good. Mine would be something bleak, like one of those adaptations of a 19th-century novel. 'Blithering Heights'?"

"Oh, come on. Your love life isn't that awkward."

"Really? I told the love of my life that I was in love with her when she had no escape from the cabin we were snowed into. I think that qualifies as at least a bit Bronte-like."

Georgie dodged the claim skillfully, avoiding the need to dig into Madelyn's feelings deeper. "If this were really something from the 19th century, wouldn't the cabin be a manor home?"

"There would probably be a governess."

"Would that be you, or me?"

Madelyn's pleasure at being caught up in a playful conversation with Georgie again overtook her. "Oh, definitely me. You'd be the glowering, mysterious manor home owner. Maybe inherited it from a distant cousin, but you never wanted to have it in the first place. Tough, hard to please. Sexy as all hell. Like a lesbian Mr. Rochester."

"Who?"

Sometimes Madelyn forgot that Georgie didn't share her academic bent, and she felt her cheeks color at the recognition she'd been flirting without meaning to. "Rich guy in a 19th-century book. Maybe a bit more like you than you'd be willing to admit."

"Does he make a mean fire, too?" Georgie pointed to the hearth. "Or is he too much of a dick to help with things?"

The pause between them sagged beneath Georgie's less-than-playful tone. Nervous sweat gathered at Madelyn's underarms.

"Can't say I remember whether he was involved in building any fires. But he's got a good heart underneath the bristly surface. That's what I meant." Madelyn ached to see Georgie retreating from the banter already.

"Ok."

"But to get back to things... Has Edmonton really been that bad? It couldn't have been all awkward."

"You underestimate my ability to make anything awkward, Mads."

"Oh, G, that's not true."

"I was joking." Georgie said the words lightly, but Madelyn could sense the deeper undercurrent of self-doubt.

"Seriously, though. It's good for you to get out there. I'm sure it's nowhere near as awkward as you think it's been."

Georgie sighed. "No, it's been pretty bad. That's the thing, Mads. I meet a girl, I kiss her, maybe fool around a bit. But when we get to talking, it's all I can do to stop myself from wishing she were you."

Had she really said that?

Madelyn's breath froze in her chest, her blood seemed to careen about her veins with wild abandon. The sound of the fire rang in her ears ten times louder than before because her whole body rioted with Georgie's words.

Though she wasn't sure what it meant yet, Madelyn's instincts screamed for it to be what she wished it was. A sign.

Hope.

"When you know someone as well as we know each other, there's, like, this rhythm. It doesn't matter if we don't see each other for a week, a month, a year or maybe even ten years—though I don't want to find out if that's true—because we fall back into the pattern without a fuss. And I don't see how I could ever reach that point with some of these women I've been hanging out with. Then I sometimes think I wouldn't want to, even if I could."

Madelyn watched through half-lowered eyelashes as Georgie's feelings spilled out of her. The normally reserved girl was nakedly vulnerable, pouring thoughts out that Madelyn felt so lucky to hear she felt tears gathering in her eyes.

"Georgie," she said. Then she hesitated, unsure of where to go from there. "I feel the same way."

Their eyes met. Madelyn's heart pounded at a comically frantic pace. She'd missed Georgie so much, wanted her nearby and wished for her to feel the love Madelyn did, that she'd mythologized a moment like this into her memory before it even happened.

Now that Georgie was admitting something about their connection, although maybe not explicitly romantic feelings, Madelyn was caught in an excited hush. Reality was turning out to be more vivid, more excruciatingly wonderful than her imagination.

Without speaking, Georgie slipped out from underneath her blankets and joined Madelyn on the couch. They snuggled up together, warming Georgie's surprisingly cool skin. Madelyn was careful not to move in a way that would jar her sore ankle, but the ice pack she'd had on her slid off.

Never mind. This was more important.

"What if I'm not meant to find love," said Georgie. "What if this is it?"

"This, as in being single? Or...us?"

"Mads, I really did need to move to Edmonton. But it doesn't feel right there, either."

"I know, you told me that you needed to. I believed you then and I believe you now. But I also believe, with every damn fiber of my body, that you're going to find what you need in life."

Georgie's sad eyes made Madelyn shift closer on the couch. She couldn't handle the pain in her friend's expression.

"How can you be so sure?"

"You know how hard it was for me to figure out my sexuality. Remember how you were crazy young? I was always so jealous of your knowing early on. You figured it out, and once you knew, you knew. No doubts, no closet, no boyfriends you couldn't quite click with."

"So, you're saying the famously indecisive one of us is the one to trust here. Wouldn't it make more sense for me to be the one who knows that I'm going to be single forever? And to be right about it?"

Georgie rolled her eyes at herself, but beneath the joking facade Madelyn knew she'd been sincere. That Georgie truly believed she was destined to remain single.

"Didn't I just tell you this week that I was in love with you? How much more could I say to combat this false notion of yours that you're doomed to be alone?"

The light outside was fading, but Georgie's eyes shone brightly in the flickering glow of the fire. When Madelyn had first told Georgie her feelings, it had gone appallingly badly. This time, speaking those words again seemed to have the opposite effect. They sank in.

"Nothing, I guess." Georgie shrugged, and in that gesture, she appeared to say so much. Madelyn's heart broke to watch her friend struggle with self-confidence like this. "I don't know why I kissed you like that earlier. I'm sorry."

Here was Madelyn's chance.

"I'm not." She stared Georgie down, not letting the fear that battered her ribcage with each manic heartbeat keep her from speaking the truth. "I'm glad you did, and I'd be glad if you did it again."

A splash of sparks shot up from the fire and Madelyn almost jumped, feeling the throb of her bad ankle bring her back to reality. But she stayed focused on Georgie, watching the way she clearly struggled with so much while saying nothing.

Before another moment could elapse, Madelyn took Georgie's hand. It was rough to the touch, worn from her welding work. But the delicate size of Georgie's finger bones surprised Madelyn. She was sure they'd held hands before, perhaps in scary movies or when comforting one another through heartbreak and pain.

Never had it felt as momentous as this.

Madelyn pulled Georgie closer so that she could kiss her again, an answer to this afternoon's tentative opening move. Georgie was tense at first, but she soon melted like a marshmallow in hot chocolate, growing softer at the edges before she let herself be completely drawn in.

This kiss was far deeper than the one earlier in the day. Madelyn felt Georgie's tongue against her lips and parted them. Eagerness swelled in her at the sensation of how entwined they became, mouths pressed up against one another, lips tingling and delicious. Her body roared with need, a flare of want so vivid she had to consciously restrain herself for fear of coming on too strong.

She didn't want to do anything Georgie would regret.

Madelyn also didn't want to close herself off from potential connection, from a pleasure she'd ached for in various ways for what now seemed like her entire life.

If Georgie wanted her, really wanted her, Madelyn would happily oblige.

There was nothing she was more certain about in this world.

Again, she felt a wave of lust wash over her, and Madelyn sparked with gratitude when Georgie shifted even closer. And then, as if her every wish were being granted all at once, Georgie's hands began to explore her body.

They had never made out before, but Madelyn had pictured it many times now. In all her fantasies, Georgie was ravenous with need for Madelyn and expressed it assertively, with skill. Real life supplanted Madelyn's feverish daydreams so quickly that it was like she'd never fantasized. Feeling Georgie touch her was that good.

A mere hand on the side of her breast sent heat directly to her center, raging with as much strength as her hottest fantasies. Georgie's other hand rested on Madelyn's hip, a steadying influence that drew her closer still.

Madelyn let herself relax into the moment, let her body feel each jolt of bliss like she might never have something this wonderful happen to her again. She knew things were tense between them, knew that Georgie would be going back to Edmonton after the cabin trip ended. There wasn't a future in place for them, at least not one they'd discussed.

And yet, that didn't matter to Madelyn just then. Her imagined monologues about taking a chance on their potential for something great evaporated in the fog of her brain. If they didn't date, so what?

At least she got to touch Georgie. Feel her touching her own body. Enjoy the sensation of how her body responded to Georgie's attention, which was both new and familiar in odd, beautiful ways.

The strength of Georgie's arms manifested in tough, wiry muscles, sleek against Madelyn's palm as she ran her hand along them. Underneath Georgie's button-up shirt, Madelyn felt her small, firm breasts and longed to see how they might goosebump at her touch.

Georgie shifted on the couch so she could kneel above Madelyn, readying herself to straddle her before she stopped, breathless, and swore.

"Oh shit. Am I hurting you?"

Madelyn's brain screamed at the way Georgie had stopped touching Madelyn. She struggled to process what the comment was even about.

"Hm?"

"Your ankle, Mads. Is it ok?"

Madelyn snorted with laughter, a release of all the pent-up tension from the past few days. Rather than answer, she pulled at Georgie's shirt collar to bring her down to another kiss.

If she'd known, all those years ago, that she'd feel this elated at kissing her best friend, Madelyn was certain she would have done it a lot earlier.

11

Age 16

Georgie stood at the edge of the high school gym in the middle of the two factions that had emerged when the lights dimmed and the music started. To her left stood the boys in overly crisp new suits, most of them ill-fitting and accessorized with gaudily bright shirts in the same colors as their dates' dresses. To the right were the girls, lip gloss visible even from meters away.

She wasn't sure what she'd been expecting. Not this. A sweater vest over her new plaid shirt had paired nicely with her Adidas sneakers when she'd gotten dressed at home. Ariel, normally catty about Georgie's boyish outfits, had even helped muss Georgie's hair just so. Here, Georgie felt like she was cosplaying as an old man who desperately clung to his youth. When she scanned the crowd of high schoolers, a few of the girls looked back nervously.

Like they were worried she might ask them to dance.

Yeah, right. You'd be lucky, she thought.

Georgie's attention studiously avoided exactly the pair of people she was most interested in. Her eyes went everywhere except where they wanted to go. Despite not looking, she could tell what was happening.

In the center of the room, bumping and dancing awkwardly beneath the rented strobe lights, were Madelyn and her date. Georgie still couldn't bring herself to consider the guy Madelyn's boyfriend, even though they'd been officially dating for a few months now.

Josh. A name as bland as his personality.

The sounds of "Live Your Life" blasted through the DJ's speaker system so loudly that Georgie felt the bass reverberate in her ribcage. It wasn't entirely unpleasant, but the song was hardly danceable, especially for a bunch of gangly teenagers hyperaware of how they looked when they moved. Some girls on the dance floor jokingly shook their asses in an exaggerated way while their dates cradled their hips like they were holding on for dear life.

Georgie sipped her plastic cup of root beer and wished she'd brought the flask she'd gotten from a friend a few weeks ago. One of the members of the GSA had a metalworker father who was surprisingly chill about underage drinking. You could get the flask personalized, even, with anything you wanted on the front. Georgie had asked for the Slytherin house logo and been thrilled to see the results.

Damn this dry dance. Alcohol-free parents' groups had organized the event.

When the song switched to "Sex on Fire," Georgie couldn't help herself. Her eyes found Madelyn on the dance floor and watched as the first few chords reached Madelyn's ears and she recognized what was playing. The glee, the shriek of excitement, were beyond endearing. Josh laughed while Madelyn took his hands and started to bounce up and down, pumped to hear her favorite song at the dance.

Madelyn danced like she truly didn't think anyone was

watching. The cliché was that you ought to, but Madelyn had no need to convince herself to live without the restrictions other people struggled with. She was entirely, completely her own person. Georgie knew this already, but seeing it that winter night at the Valentine's Day dance confirmed her beliefs even more.

It hurt too much to watch. That, she also knew. But it was like watching a car slide on a patch of ice to an inevitable crash. Looking away was unthinkable because she was bound to the results, horrified. So Georgie stood there nodding her head and watching Josh and Madelyn dance. Madelyn's boundless joy at the chorus, the drums, everything was so heart-piercingly pure that Georgie felt her throat constrict.

She knew she had to get over how she felt.

That didn't make it any easier.

How could Madelyn ever love her back, when Madelyn was straight? Hope had buoyed Georgie's spirits for a while, bargaining that maybe Madelyn was bisexual or still figuring things out. But as she gazed at Madelyn smiling into Josh's sweaty teenaged face, Georgie couldn't see how anyone would tolerate having Josh's hands on her body without being 100%, completely heterosexual.

Technically, there was nothing wrong with him. He played guitar, badly, and liked the sound of his own voice a bit more than Georgie cared to hear, but he was a good enough person. Josh's most incriminating flaw was simply that he was not Georgie, and by getting in between Georgie and the girl she loved, he had exposed a fatal miscalculation in Georgie's assumptions.

Therefore, it was while watching Josh's gormless expression as he danced, the tiniest bite of his lip the only indication that he was concentrating on what happened around him, that Georgie felt she had finally put up with enough. She and Madelyn were still close, but they were drifting.

It was time to cut the cord and sail away.

Time to go.

Except that at the same moment as Georgie realized she had to focus her affections elsewhere, Madelyn spotted Georgie at the edge of the gym.

"Georgie! You came!" she shrieked, bounding over to her like Josh wasn't even there. Georgie found herself enveloped in a typical Madelyn hug: all-consuming, long-lasting, and a little too much.

"Yeah, wasn't much on TV," Georgie heard herself say. The ringing in her ears could have been the volume of the DJ's music, but she suspected it had more to do with close physical proximity to her crush. Not that the word 'crush' came anywhere near explaining what she felt for Madelyn.

"I'm so glad you made it," Madelyn said, beaming as she held a hand on Georgie's shoulder. The touch lingered and Georgie shrugged it off, finally, unable to stand the contact if it weren't a sign of romantic intent.

The silhouette of Josh ambled over, nodding at Georgie with a placid smile while he draped an arm around Madelyn's shoulders. "Hey."

"Hey, man," said Georgie.

"Josh! Isn't this amazing? Never thought I'd see the day. Georgie at a dance!"

"Looking pretty hipster, G-money," said Josh. She bristled at the unwanted nickname.

Better than your shiny turquoise dress shirt, Joshua.

Georgie bit her tongue, though. Madelyn had been so embarrassed when she told Georgie that she had a boyfriend. Like she'd needed to apologize, or something. Georgie had assured her that they could talk about things like boys, that just because she was gay didn't mean she hated helping her friend with problems.

Too bad she'd been a little less than honest when she said that.

Though, seen in another light, the issue wasn't that Georgie was gay. She could have been the dykiest girl in all of Western Canada and had no problem with girl talk sessions if she hadn't had those pesky feelings of hers. The ones that woke her in the night from restless, sweaty dreams where Madelyn slipped into her bed.

"I try," Georgie said to Josh. She rolled her eyes at Madelyn, hoping it conveyed the frustration she felt with enough amusement to keep things light. She and Madelyn often talked about how the term 'hipster' was a stupid insult used by people threatened by someone different from them.

"Come on, come dance with us!" Madelyn said breathily. A sheen of sweat made her skin glow in the strobing lights, and though Georgie hated dancing almost as much as she disliked Josh, she had to admit that both feelings were rooted in deeply unfair bias. Plus, what else was she going to do?

"Fine, fine."

"Oooh shit, this is my jam!" yelped Josh, his voice breaking slightly as he spoke. The song that came on was Coldplay. Georgie fought the urge to roll her eyes at Madelyn again. She mostly succeeded, but beneath her significant restraint she wondered what Madelyn could possibly see in this guy. He was like a walking boredom machine.

Though the song wasn't bad, by any means, Georgie wasn't moved to dance through passion for the music. She shuffled, bopping her head along to the beat, while Madelyn tried to dance between Georgie and Josh, spending time looking at each of them equally. The artifice of the situation made her attempt all the sweeter.

Georgie knew she should appreciate the lengths to which her friend would go to try to make her feel welcome and comfortable. Hell, Madelyn had joined the GSA alongside Georgie and proudly wore her Ally pin, even to the most redneck of places. Hannah and Nadia, Georgie's new queer friends who were already dating when she had started going to GSA meetings, had welcomed Madelyn into the fold. It did help, a bit.

Nothing could make things turn out the way Georgie wanted, though.

It only took the one song to show her that. And it wasn't that Madelyn paid too much attention to Josh—though any amount was more than Georgie felt he deserved—so much as that Georgie didn't want to be a third wheel with her own soulmate.

At least, she'd thought Madelyn was her soulmate.

Maybe Georgie was just another girl falling for the wrong person.

While the song faded and another rose up to take its place, Georgie slipped away from the dance floor and trotted out the gymnasium doors. The fluorescent hallway lights hurt her eyes while she adjusted to the brightness, but as the sound of the music faded and turned into a muted bump and bass, she felt her heartbeat slow.

“G! Wait!"

Madelyn's voice arrested her, as it always did.

"Georgie!"

She'd kept walking, but the sound of Madelyn clacking down the floor in her borrowed high heels made her turn despite herself.

"Why are you leaving? You just got here."

"I know. But I've gotta go."

For countless weeks following the Valentine's Day dance, Georgie would wish she'd had more courage that night. She would castigate herself for her many failings, her weaknesses that determined the course of the talk with Madelyn. Because instead of telling her how she felt, she bottled the emotion even more tightly.

If she was going to be in love with her best friend, that was her business, and no one else's. She might be wallowing in self-pity and shame, but at least she'd have the dignity of no one else knowing that was the case. She hadn't even told Nadia and Hannah. Georgie's mind was set in the split-second it took for Madelyn's earnest face to shift to a frown.

"What's wrong?"

Georgie knew she should have been honest. Trust was the foundation of a close friendship, after all. Still, deep down she didn't believe she could tell Madelyn what she felt without losing her completely. So she kept her secret buried and spoke lies, instead.

The words Georgie hissed at Madelyn weren't completely dishonest. They had a base layer of truth to them, but the focus was all wrong. If her feelings were an iceberg, then Georgie only lashed out with the top layer visible. Only discussed that crisp, icy tip of things, pretending that what lurked beneath didn't exist at all.

"Come on, Madelyn. You know what's wrong. I came here to have fun at the dance, just like you begged me to. But you're so distracted with Josh. It's not like it used to be, back when we were friends in middle school. You don't have time for me anymore."

The obvious hurt in Madelyn's face melted Georgie's heart. Her guts wavered, screaming for her to speak what was actually going on. But the willful, stubborn brain calling the shots squashed any dissent and continued on its trajectory.

"I thought you said it was ok for me to be dating him."

They were standing in the front entrance to their high school, beneath the rows of sports trophies from generations prior to theirs, the muffled sounds of the dance the only accompaniment to their words. Above them, a fluorescent tube flickered in its panel.

"Yeah. That's not the point. You said things wouldn't change between us, but they obviously have. I only came here because you wanted me to. Nadia and Hannah were going to go to Jessie's Diner."

It was characteristic of Madelyn that she took the burden of responsibility entirely on herself. No blame for Georgie seemed to occur to her. That alone should have been reason for Georgie to lay off her fury, but somehow it only fanned the flames.

"I'm sorry, G. Do you want to go back inside, and we can request a song you'd like to dance to? Josh can get us some more drinks."

"You know I don't like dancing. What's the point?"

"Please, it's been a while since we've hung out. We could just eat candy on the sidelines?"

The hope in Madelyn's eyes was emphasized by her makeup. She looked lovely, and though Georgie longed to say so, she'd repressed so much already. What was one more thing?

"No, I can't. I'm going to go."

Georgie left her best friend standing outside the Valentine's Day dance, crying rivulets down her perfect, rosy cheeks. For no good reason. Georgie had pushed just for the sake of pushing, hurt Madelyn to avoid a deeper hurt if she revealed how she actually felt. Sick roiling in her gut announced that she'd made a terrible decision.

As if that wasn't already obvious to Georgie.

She stamped outside, shivering in the fluffy snow while she made her way to her beater of a car. With the ignition turned on, the car's tape deck started blaring Black Flag at a volume that annoyed anyone unlucky enough to be her passenger. But Georgie didn't put the car into gear. Not yet.

She sat in the driver's seat, listening to the raucous punk music and staring at her phone.

Should say something. Tell Madelyn it's not her fault.

Georgie typed out a message, painstakingly making her way through the T9 predictive text to apologize. "Sorry. Not feeling like myself tonight, but it's not your fault. I shouldn't have gotten so angry. I hope you have fun, and you look beautiful tonight."

The words glowed on her screen, but they looked so dumb. Inadequate. Before she could gather the courage to press send, she deleted everything. There weren't the right words to say what she wanted to, so better to say nothing than that shit.

Just as she was about to put her phone in the cup holder and reverse out of her spot, the phone buzzed.

It was Madelyn.

She'd written "You mean so much to me, Georgie. Please take care of yourself tonight. Xoxo, Mads."

And though her body was raging and her music was furious, all Georgie felt was complete despair. She melted onto the steering wheel and tears poured out of her faster than she could stop them. With frenetic power chords as her backdrop, she let herself sob out every feeling she couldn't give voice to.

12

Present Day

How was this happening?

Madelyn recalled, distinctly, the moment she realized she loved Georgie. It was during a bath after softball practice, when she inspected a bruise on the side of her thigh and thought about how much time she'd spent hating that part of her body. Too soft, too willing to jiggle when exposed in shorts, too pale and squishy and cellulite-dappled.

And she'd remembered the abrupt, aggressive laugh Georgie had burst into when Madelyn first told Georgie she hated her thighs. Madelyn had been so offended, sure that Georgie was laughing at her for feeling insecure. But it came out, in further conversation, that Georgie had thought Madelyn was being ironic. Satirizing women's insecurities about thighs because they were like a Cathy comic come to life.

It hadn't occurred to Georgie that Madelyn could feel so negatively about her body, and she'd said so. "Because you're perfect," she'd said.

Madelyn had prodded her thigh bruise in the bath and

felt her chest swell with affection at the memory. Georgie thought she was perfect. But how could Madelyn be the perfect one? Wasn't that Georgie?

Madelyn had stayed in the bathwater past its warmth. As the water cooled, she lost herself in thought. Perhaps it would be more accurate to call it feeling, not thought, for she swelled with all kinds of sentimental memories. Suddenly, shivers caught up to her and she leapt from the tub.

The face that stared back from Madelyn's bathroom mirror hardly seemed like her own. In those eyes, the same ones that had confronted her every time she'd looked in a reflective surface since childhood, she saw something new. A spark. If it had been there longer than she realized, so what? At least she saw it now.

Madelyn was in love.

She didn't look different in any noticeable way, but her reflection appeared to quiver at the edges. Something deep within her had shifted and though all her molecules, muscles, and feelings were the same, they existed in a completely different context. The chill from a too-long bath began to move her from surreal to outright cold, so she wrapped herself in a towel and had a good, long cry.

It had been so cathartic.

Madelyn was no longer sure what she'd hoped Georgie would say when she told her how she felt. Those daydreams in the months before the trip, on the drive out to Banff, crumbled under scrutiny. Instead, Madelyn now looked into Georgie's eyes, the tip of Georgie's nose a little pink from the power outage's effects on the cabin, and grinned.

"I'm so glad I met you," she murmured. There was no time for more words, though, because Madelyn dove into another kiss. Georgie's mouth was far too enticing. Her effect on Madelyn was strong, a bright, clear spot in a murky and vast world.

Though Georgie didn't respond out loud, the pace of her kissing rose to a new level. Her hand was tightly wound in the back of Madelyn's hair, cradling the nape of her neck while bringing her nearer. They could have melded into one person just then. Madelyn was certain she'd never felt so intimately close to someone before.

Crackling sparks in the fire formed a background symphony that painted bright spots in Madelyn's eyes. Nothing shone more than Georgie, though. She shrugged off the button-up shirt covering her tank top, revealing the smooth, strong lines of her arms. Madelyn's body screamed internally at how alluring Georgie looked.

Rather than voicing those feelings, Madelyn let her fingers trail down from Georgie's face to the edges of her shoulder, her triceps. Not only did Georgie pull Madelyn closer, but her toned body rippled with energy that seemed to hum beneath the surface of her skin. It was all Madelyn could do to restrain herself from laughing at the wonderful absurdity of her situation.

Georgie, her friend, was the one she was touching. And it wasn't just some casual brush against one another in the hallway. Madelyn delighted in every inch more exploration Georgie allowed her, and she felt her excitement rise ever higher as she did so.

If it wasn't for that excitement, she wouldn't have gone further. What she did next surprised Madelyn almost as much as realizing she loved Georgie. With a swift, decisive motion, she took off her top, revealing a simple black bra hugging her delicate breasts. Rather than shy away from Georgie's gaze, she stared and enjoyed the feeling of her attention. Her hunger.

Goosebumps rose on Madelyn's skin while she sat there. It felt like eons, but Georgie moved to pull down one of the bra's cups and lick Madelyn's nipple in what must have been only a few seconds. The rest of Madelyn's sense of time was obliterated as Georgie's tongue met flesh.

Oh sweet fresh hell, thought Madelyn.

What she actually said was a consonant-free moan, the nature of which was clear. Georgie had awakened something deep within Madelyn that couldn't be contained. Not tonight. She wondered, then, if anything in Georgie was feeling the same way. The pace at which she paid attention to Madelyn's breasts seemed to say yes.

Warmth continued to grow in Madelyn's core, singing a deep note of longing that rang out across her body. With a soft grunt, Madelyn freed herself entirely of her bra and let Georgie have access to her, unencumbered. It was only moments before she used this newfound luck to tweak Madelyn's nipple hard enough to make her gasp.

"Oh, I like that sound," murmured Georgie. She looked surprised at the huskiness of her own voice, but that shock didn't bar her from tugging at Madelyn's jeans, the two of them wriggling on the couch awkwardly before sliding in a heap to the floor.

“Shit. Is your ankle ok?” Georgie asked. She pulled one of the blankets from the couch and repositioned herself on it before the fire.

Something made Madelyn pause.

"Are you sure we should do this?"

A cloud seemed to pass over Georgie's expression, but it faded so quickly Madelyn wasn't sure she'd even seen it. Firelight flickered behind Georgie, casting all kinds of unreliable and ephemeral shadows.

"Are you?" asked Georgie.

Deep inside Madelyn, a voice that knew logic and caution prepared itself to speak. But its throat-clearing was timid, uncertain. A much louder answer thrummed in Madelyn's veins. The setting was romantic, the person ideal, the thronging ache inside her ripe.

"I've wanted this for so long," Madelyn said quietly. "Yes."

"Sounds good," Georgie answered. Her voice was hushed, and the tone was filled with unabashed lust. But Madelyn thought she also heard emotion in it, real, passionate feeling that demonstrated she wasn't entirely wrong about confessing her love to Georgie. Maybe there was something worth exploring between them.

If that could be the case...it felt too good to be true.

Georgie's hands on Madelyn also felt good, but they were categorically, obviously there. No need for introspection to understand how they caused explosions of want inside her. Madelyn wanted Georgie more than she'd ever wanted anyone before.

She did what her body screamed at her to do, she rid herself of every remaining stitch of clothing. The air wasn't as cold as she'd worried it would be. Not now, with lust crackling between them as vividly as the fire. Not when Georgie shed her clothes, too, and wrapped her arm around Madelyn, her free hand roving down to touch her.

Georgie was tentative at first, though clearly skilled. It wasn't for lack of sexual experience that she seemed to hesitate. Madelyn hoped, perhaps illogically, that this meant as much to Georgie as it did to her. That could explain the way Georgie's fingers danced on her skin like they were afraid to leave any sign of their presence.

"Harder is ok," whispered Madelyn. "Pressure works for me."

They made eye contact while Georgie listened to Madelyn's instruction, and then followed suit, gauging her reaction until she found the perfect stroke. Then Madelyn's attention faltered, and she found her eyelids fluttering closed against her wishes. It felt too good; she had no choice.

She grasped Georgie, kissing her when she could rally the strength to focus on something other than her own pleasure, but Madelyn's body had begun to shiver and buck with delight at what was occurring. Before long, Georgie let fingers slide into Madelyn's eager, waiting opening.

A gasp.

"Too soon?" asked Georgie. The care she showed Madelyn made new sparks tingle down Madelyn's spine. This was no ordinary hook-up. Something was shifting between them, sands blowing from one dune to another that reformed into a completely different landscape.

Madelyn shook her head and smiled. "Just soon enough."

She relaxed into the feeling and allowed herself to make as much noise as she wanted. They were, after all, stranded. Alone. Completely muffled by huge drifts of snow, insulation as beautiful and picturesque as it could be deadly. Georgie's tongue joined her hands in concert and she focused entirely on Madelyn.

Without another thought surfacing, Madelyn sank into a deep, thigh-shaking satisfaction that rolled through her like a thunderstorm. Georgie guided her, watched her, held her. It was an orgasm like no other.

Madelyn was surprised she'd come so quickly, given she normally had to coax pleasure out of herself with a carefully arranged set of prerequisites. Georgie must have connected with her on a completely different level.

Of course she had.

It was another sign, thought Madelyn. *Of how they belonged.*

With this possibility in her mind, Madelyn rolled over to switch places with Georgie and brought blankets with her.

Georgie laughed. "You need a cocoon?"

"I'm cold."

"Maybe should have thought of that before you got naked."

"Mmm, no," said Madelyn, nuzzling Georgie's neck. She traced lines along the hipbones rising from Georgie's torso. "Because then I don't know if I would have. And that was amazing."

Rather than answer with words, Georgie pulled Madelyn down into another kiss. They tumbled together, lips ravenous for each other, thighs intertwined and fingers grasping with such a need Madelyn surprised herself. She'd never believed her animal nature could feel so apparent.

Wrestling, it felt like. The best kind. One of them would push the other to the brink, hold back for a second, and then dive in again to hear shouts of pleasure ring out in the vaulted log ceiling. Time passed like a floating cloud.

Madelyn was lost in Georgie's firm stomach, deliberating over the structure of her ab muscles, when she should have heard it. Another kiss deepened her denial to what was happening. Fever, heat, and utter disregard for anything but sex, Georgie, and the present kept Madelyn unaware.

Her senses were filled with Georgie, with the absolute, lightheaded bliss of being able to enjoy her body and her attention this way. So Madelyn didn't notice the footsteps on the front deck, muffled as they were by the heaps of snow. Voices should have been audible, too, but a moan was a curious thing that dampened everything else in the air.

Then she heard something. They talked about it briefly,

interrupting their bliss with heart-pounding uncertainty. Too late.

The door was opening—the front door—and people spilled inside, friends. Faces she recognized. "Hi!" she said, before her brain could process what was happening.

Georgie clutched the blankets around her body, suddenly shy like her childhood self. Madelyn's mind struggled to keep up with what was happening, still crying out angrily that pleasures had been taken from it.

"Oh my god!" yelled Hannah. She pointed at the two naked figures with obvious glee. "I fucking knew it!"

"You know, we rushed up here to make sure you two weren't stranded without food or help or whatever, but it doesn't look like you were struggling at all," said Nadia. She set down a box of supplies and opened the door to speak to some other person. "No rush, they're just fucking."

"Seriously? Don't pretend you're not happy about this," said Hannah. "Is this just cause I bet you $20 that one time they'd hook up?"

Georgie scrambled into her shirt and pants, the disheveled hair at the back of her head all the more endearing when clothed. "You had a bet going?"

"Yeah, that's not cool," Madelyn said. She clung to the blanket hiding her naked body from their friends. Embarrassment radiated off Georgie, but though Madelyn wished they hadn't been caught in the act, she was still glad it had happened.

"Did everyone except me think this was an inevitability?" asked Georgie. The edge to her voice wiped the smile off Hannah's face.

"It was a long time ago. Like a bet you make over beers one night, not serious," said Nadia. As if her matter-of-fact explanation could quell all of Georgie's fears.

But Madelyn saw that Georgie's muscles were tensing even more. She edged closer to Georgie, reaching out a hand to touch her arm, and Georgie shrugged her off violently.

"I don't mean the bet, I mean the whole thing. If you all thought this for so long why didn't you tell me?"

Another tromping set of footsteps drew closer and the door to the cabin opened. It was a man, who dusted the snow from his jeans and looked with surprise at the scenario unfolding.

"Cold in here, jeez. Everything ok, folks?" he asked Hannah.

"Fine, thanks," hissed Hannah. "Thank you again for the ride up here."

"Who's he?" Madelyn said, still reeling from the sudden change of everything she'd pictured happening that night. One minute she'd been sure that she and Georgie would spend the evening wrapped in each other's arms, talking about feelings between sessions of lovemaking. The next, their friends had burst in and thrown everything off.

"We hitched a ride with the guy driving the snowplow up the road here. Left the car in town because the mountain roads are still so bad," Nadia answered. "but we're good now. Thanks." The man backed out of the cabin, his face a hilarious picture of having wandered into drama he didn't ask for.

"Is no one going to answer my question?" Georgie looked accusingly at the faces surrounding her, moving from one to the next with a furrowed brow and searching eyes.

"I'm sure they didn't mean it that way, Georgie," said Madelyn. "More just, you know, that we've been close for forever. Sometimes people ship best friends."

"You can't 'ship' real people!" Georgie said, her exasperated sigh causing an immediate pang to rise up in Madelyn's throat. Their bubble of intimacy had been resoundingly pierced.

"Sure you can," piped up Nadia. "People do it all the time with celebrities."

"Well, I'd appreciate not being treated like someone who asked to be in the public eye. Keep your shit to yourselves. I'm going back to Banff with the plow driver—don't let him leave before I've gotten my things."

Georgie started grabbing belongings desperately, flinging them into a makeshift pile in front of her boots while the rest of them looked on in surprise. Her mood had shifted so suddenly that no one else could keep up.

"Woah, Georgie, we didn't mean anything serious by it," Hannah said. "I'm sorry."

"Yeah, we just got here. Don't let us ruin things for you," added Nadia.

Madelyn walked closer, her bare feet tingling on the cold floor. "Georgie," she said, her voice soft so that only Georgie could hear her. "You're obviously hurt. Can you stay so we can talk about this? Please?"

Judging by the way Georgie fumed, Madelyn wasn't confident her words had any effect. The plea was earnest, verging on desperate, but she couldn't lose Georgie's attention just as she was gaining it. Everything else about the cabin rental had gone awry; she couldn't handle it if the most important part of her plans completely backfired.

“Fine. I’m going to bed," muttered Georgie. She strode upstairs and sequestered herself in the bedroom she'd claimed when she first arrived at the cabin. When the door shut, loudly, a sputtering noise hummed through the building for a brief second. And then the power flickered on.

As the lights began to shine again, the stove clock blinked its fluorescent numbers in an even pace, and other appliances began to chirp and beep their way back into life. Madelyn stood, smiling despite herself, wondering at the bizarre and sometimes agonizing turns to this Banff trip.

She knew trying to talk to Georgie now would only infuriate her. Though Madelyn craved to fix all Georgie's problems, space was likely what her friend needed. With Nadia and Hannah here, they could return to the normal pace of things. So she stalled her urges and tried to calm down.

"Anyone else need a drink?" she asked Nadia and Hannah. When they laughed and nodded, Madelyn excused herself for a moment to get dressed, and then returned to crack open a bottle of Prosecco.

13

After a few hours of catching up with Nadia and Hannah, discussing the power outage, her hurt ankle, and some, though not all, of the events with Georgie, Madelyn returned upstairs to her bedroom drowsily. Sleep called to her so loudly that she flung herself into the bed without taking off her clothes.

She was unconscious and resting for a few hours, her body claiming its much-needed downtime to mend her ankle. Perhaps it also needed to recuperate from expending so much energy during sex. But in the middle of the night, Madelyn's eyes fluttered open. The darkness was still complete, the cabin forest-nestled and wintry.

She'd had a dream, though, that roused her from sleep. Upon waking, Madelyn didn't remember what had happened. She only knew that she had to talk to Georgie. Ideally, now. Even she could tell, though, that waking her in the dark, trapping her into a conversation yet again, wasn't a good idea.

Madelyn stayed in her bedroom, composing thoughts into sentences, and then paragraphs, that she could speak out loud when morning came. If she'd bungled the first 'love' discussion, she'd be damn sure she didn't mess up the second. Especially not with Georgie's feelings so tender from the others arriving, amused by the situation they'd found them in.

When the darkness shifted to a purple-toned steely first light, Madelyn stretched, exploring the range of motion she could manage with her ankle. It wasn't as sore as yesterday now. From her bed, she heard the day beginning, with subtle sounds creeping into being.

A few seemed to come from inside the cabin. It took Madelyn longer than it should have to identify that the noises were that of someone sneaking out of a room, quietly down the stairs, and out the door. When she heard the latch click in the front, she leapt out of bed and hobbled herself into the hall.

"Georgie?" she called out quietly.

She could see a figure outside, surrounded by the early morning darkness of winter. Though vision alone couldn't confirm that it was Georgie, her heart knew that it was. She was trying to escape. Just as Georgie had run to Edmonton, away from Calgary, away from her, she was now using her favorite method to avoid deeper conversation.

Or maybe it was just to avoid the humiliation of having their friends know they were working on something emotional and non-platonic.

Whatever the reason, the figure waded down the snowy front steps while Madelyn staggered along the indoor staircase. She would have moved faster, could probably have caught her, if she hadn't had a hurt ankle. Pain keened at her now, but she pushed it down.

She hadn't come all this way, gone through all the tumult of the last few days, to lose her shot. Madelyn needed Georgie to know that she wanted to be with her, whatever their friends thought. Underneath the harrowing anxiety of watching her best friend, her love, run away from difficult interactions, Madelyn suspected that Georgie felt the same way.

If not the same, at least similar.

Hopefully similar.

Madelyn shook her head. To be honest with herself, she had no idea how Georgie felt. For all she knew, their tryst in the cabin yesterday had been the product of boredom and garden variety lust on Georgie's part. She hadn't said anything about love.

That had all been Madelyn.

Doubt sapped the last of Madelyn's resolve at the same time as the sound of an engine sputtering to life met Madelyn's ears. Georgie's truck's lights cut into the darkness, suddenly illuminating the trees with grotesque shadows, the cast of light as cold as the winter's air. Madelyn reached the main floor and watched, exhausted, as Georgie took out her emergency gear shovel and began to excavate the truck enough to move it.

For a minute, Madelyn stood watching Georgie work. Her shovel scooped piles of heavy snow at a pace that revealed Georgie's desperation to leave this place. It made Madelyn wonder whether she should intervene at all. Perhaps it would be best to finally stop meddling.

But that's never been me, thought Madelyn.

And with stakes sky-high, she wasn't about to become someone new. Not now. Not with Georgie on the line.

Madelyn shrugged on a coat, leaving the front unzipped, and stepped into a pair of boots that didn't belong to her. Ownership didn't matter before 9:00 a.m. when love was at risk. Especially not in the dead of winter.

"Georgie!" said Madelyn. She had to raise her voice to speak over the drone of Georgie's engine, the hefting shovelfuls of snow adding to the noise periodically.

Georgie looked up, her cheeks and nose flushed with exertion, while her truck kept rumbling. She'd dug out a good trench along the driver's side now, and the departure of the plow driver's vehicle last night had left tracks behind her where she could escape.

Madelyn couldn't let that happen.

"What are you doing awake right now?" asked Georgie.

"I could say the same to you, G."

"Gotta dig this out. I can't stay."

"Why not?" Madelyn said, edging closer. If she moved too quickly, her ankle might buckle. She wanted to appear strong. Composed. Something rational that Georgie could respect. So she shuffled, her heart rate elevated from the work of making her way through snow.

There were only a few more steps to go before Madelyn would be on level ground. Only a few feet after that to get to Georgie, who braced herself with shoulders hunched to scoop another shovel's worth of snow.

"Georgie, I said why not?"

Georgie pushed the shovel into the drift near her truck's back tire aggressively, the action venting a thick burst of emotion.

"Why not? Madelyn, come on. I can't do this. You know me, I'm not a public, touchy-feely kind of person. It's bad enough to get snowed in on our vacation, but bad takes on another level when I've gotta think about spending another few days with those ones gossiping about me."

Georgie nodded towards the cabin as she spoke, her eyebrows furrowed so that you wouldn't have guessed she was talking about friends. Good friends, ones she'd known for years.

"They're not the ones I need you to stay for. Please, I need to talk to you. We need to talk. Work through things," said Madelyn.

"What's there to say?"

Madelyn gripped the coat around herself tighter, wishing she'd brought mittens outside. The raw pink chill of her fingers began to numb far deeper than the skin.

"You know that I care about you. And what happened yesterday, it wasn't how it should have gone, maybe, but I'm still glad it happened. Even if Nadia and Hannah interrupted us, I can't tell you how much it means to—"

"Maybe? Of course it's not how it should have gone. You think every little girl grows up dreaming about how her first time with someone will be on the floor? Will be witnessed by people laughing about it?"

"Your first time? I thought you'd had lots of sex before... you told me about it when it happened." Madelyn chewed on her lip. A pit of abject fear had begun growing in her belly. There was so much she hadn't seen, hadn't known. It might be too late now.

"Jesus, Mads! I'm not a virgin. I just mean, the first time with someone new. It's supposed to be special. Supposed to, I don't know, fuck it. I'm going home to get over myself. We can talk later." Georgie finished shoveling the snow out from around the truck and threw the shovel back into the rear cab seats.

Madelyn was running out of time.

"You're angry. I get that, Georgie. Really, I do. It wasn't cool of them to laugh and act like it's all so predictable. If I'd known years ago that this was how I felt, it would have saved so much time and heartbreak."

"Too bad you're late to the big gay party, right?"

"No!"

"I can't do this, Mads. I'm sorry," Georgie said. She hopped into the front seat of the truck in a swift motion. Before she could close the door, before all hope of reconciliation was lost, Madelyn managed to shout:

"I'm not late to the party, I'm just late to you. Please—"

But the closure of the truck door cut short her words, and Georgie shifted into reverse quickly and decisively. She drove into the countryside road at a pace that would have made Madelyn grip her seat nervously, and then Georgie sped off alone. Flurries of snow fell off the truck as she drove away.

Madelyn stood, shivering, wondering how many more times she'd fuck up her life this week. There wasn't much more time left before the holidays were over. Thank god.

The morning's events hadn't woken anyone but Madelyn. She shuffled back inside with an impossibly heavy heart, the corners of her mouth wobbling with the desire to cry. Still, if she succumbed to the feeling, there would be no saving her from her sadness. And her friends had only just arrived last night.

Rather than focus on the pain she was feeling emotionally, Madelyn thought it best to warm herself up from standing in the cold without proper winter gear. She started and tended a large fire, pushing the left couch even closer so she could sink onto it and bask in the warmth.

Had she invented her suspicion that Georgie felt something for her? It had been a long time since they'd seen each other in person. Distance could warp things. Time could blunt your perception. And yet Madelyn felt, deep within her solar plexus, a spark resided in her that had responded to something similar within Georgie. Kinship.

It had taken a long time to get there, but Madelyn had known Georgie for as long as she could remember knowing people. They were closer than most people ever got to have friends. If most of her prominent childhood and adolescent memories were of this person, didn't she know Georgie at least as well as your average passer-by?

If not whole oceans' worth of depth more?

So how could Georgie make her feel so good, share in such an intimate act as they had experienced, and leave without so much as a discussion of what that meant? To Madelyn's academic mind, which delighted in lengthy dissections of words and meanings, it was unthinkable.

She let the fire die down and then went upstairs for a bath. Now that the power was back on, the water heater would function again. Madelyn sat on the edge of the tub watching the water fill it, still unable to stop thinking of Georgie. Her kiss, her voracious attentions.

When Madelyn lowered herself into the water, she saw her naked body in a new light. It was no longer just the physical form that she carted around, but something more. Here was where Georgie had licked so softly that Madelyn hadn't been sure she'd made contact with her skin. There was a light bruise from the ecstatic grasp on her hip while Georgie cried out and came.

A map of their intimacy stretched out before Madelyn in that bath, and she found herself in tears. Fat droplets streamed down her face to join the bathwater, and she let herself sob through a full half hour of soaking. When the water began to cool, Madelyn composed herself and stood to dress again.

Confronting the red-eyed reflection in the mirror wasn't easy.

"You've done this all wrong," she said to herself. "Dumbass."

Like she couldn't have just made plans to visit Georgie in Edmonton, talking with her there instead of at their yearly group vacation.

With a sigh, Madelyn finished dressing and left the bathroom, a steamy hot wall of air dissipating behind her as she went. She nearly tripped over Hannah when she reached the hall.

"Hey Madelyn," said Hannah. "Have you seen Georgie?" Hannah's voice was tender; she'd clearly heard Madelyn crying.

Madelyn had meant to stay calm. Her plan had been to enjoy her friends' company, to shelve her feelings for once and let the day proceed without obsessing over Georgie. Hannah and Nadia deserved to have a vacation. So did she.

Plans melt easily when emotions wash over them.

"Yes," said Madelyn, her voice breaking slightly. Hannah knew, without asking a single question, that Madelyn was distressed.

"You need a hug?" she said, starting the embrace before Madelyn could answer, saving her the necessity of a sob breaking through her words. Instead, Madelyn let her tears stain the purple shirt Hannah wore emblazoned with rainbow-colored twenty-sided dice.

"I'm sorry," Madelyn said. Hannah just patted her back, letting her feel the things she was trying so desperately to repress.

Embarrassment. Longing. A tinge of anger, though she wasn't sure if it were directed more at herself or at Georgie.

Maybe at life in general.

Why couldn't they have synced up? Why couldn't they be together?

Madelyn didn't have the answers, but she reminded herself, wrapped in the warm arms of a friend, that she did have people who cared about her. She composed herself and went downstairs with Hannah, where they met the smells and sounds of a brunch-cooking Nadia.

"You're up!" said Nadia, grinning at Madelyn. "Took you long enough."

"Nah, she was there when Georgie left this morning," said Hannah, filling in the gaps for Madelyn so she didn't have to. Madelyn wanted to hug Hannah again to thank her for this kindness. "We were the ones who slept in."

"Ugh," groaned Nadia, "couldn't Georgie at least have told us she was heading out? I know we ribbed her pretty good last night, but Georgie used to be able to take as well as she gave."

Awkward silence hung in the moment that followed. Nadia constantly made dirty jokes, but in the anemic morning sunshine she seemed to be holding back. Then Madelyn caught Nadia's eye and Nadia snorted with laughter.

"Maybe Madelyn can tell us whether that's true now or not. Mads, you have a good time together?"

Madelyn smiled shyly, feeling the hot flush in her cheeks with a sense of pride. She was here, safe with friends, even if her chest hurt more than she thought physically possible—short of an actual heart attack.

"A lady doesn't kiss and tell," she said, smiling in a way she hoped was mysterious.

"I think a lady also doesn't get caught literally naked mid-sex in front of a fireplace, Madelyn," said Hannah as she raised an eyebrow.

Madelyn sat down at the island, leaning on her elbows while she glanced from Nadia to Hannah.

"It was nice," she said. "Really nice."

"I always did think you two would hook up," Hannah added. "No joke."

"Yeah, it's been clear that Georgie's been carrying a torch for you for years," Nadia said.

"Wait. Really?" Madelyn's cheeks flushed again. She felt the heat of embarrassment go much deeper this time. How dumb not to have noticed.

Though Hannah was less categorical in her statements, Madelyn could tell from their hesitant eye contact, their restrained smiles, that this was something they'd discussed before. It wasn't just in her head.

It wasn't just in her head!

From shame to hope in thirty seconds flat, Madelyn's heart reeled. She noticed that her palms left damp spots on the island's surface and laughed, too loud, at the realization.

"Are you ok?" asked Nadia. "Did you hit your head when you hurt your ankle?"

Hannah snorted, but Nadia wasn't joking.

"I'm good," said Madelyn. "In fact, maybe I'm better than I've been in a long time."

Because for the first time in months, Madelyn's feverish thoughts weren't echoing around in her head, alone. They were out there in the world. She'd told Georgie how she felt. And though Georgie hadn't reacted as she'd hoped she would, now there were others attesting to what Madelyn had felt to be true.

If only Georgie hadn’t just made it seem very clear she couldn’t be what Madelyn needed.

14

AGE 19

"She's late," said Quinn, her arms folded across her chest. Her sharp green eyes darted to the coffee shop door each time someone entered. None, so far, had been Madelyn. A wave of guilt rushed over Georgie for feeling relieved.

"That's pretty much Madelyn in a nutshell," she said to Quinn. "She's not trying to bug you. I promise."

"It's so inconsiderate. She knows we're supposed to meet at 10:00, so why can't she just plan to get here early if she's always late? That'd cancel itself out. She'd be here on time."

"You're thinking like Quinn, and not like Madelyn, babe. If she knew she was going to be early, it'd cancel itself out the wrong way. Like, 'oh, I have even more time than usual, so I'm ok.' Until, next thing you know it, she's more late than normal."

Quinn cradled Georgie's hand underneath the table, their thumbs vying for the top spot. When Quinn looked into Georgie's eyes, the reaction in Georgie's stomach was so powerful she forgot, for a second, what they were doing.

All she could focus on was this beautiful girl sitting next

to her. Who wasn't just beautiful, but sexy, smart, and super funny. Weirdest of all, she thought the same things of Georgie.

How come she hadn't gotten a girlfriend before this?

University was a great place to meet women, truth be told. Georgie had slept around a little at first, eager to stretch her baby dyke wings and get out of the rut of high school. Here, she was an adult. Independent. Had moved far past the stereotypes of her teenaged cohort, scared as most of them were of her sexuality.

It had taken a bit of time for Georgie to be willing to commit, even a little. Quinn was her first actual, 'do you want to be my girlfriend?' experience. And each wrinkle of that perfect little nose made her so glad she'd asked.

Except just now, Quinn wasn't wrinkling her nose from amusement. That was definitely a sneer. Strange defensiveness gathered in Georgie's chest when she saw the object of Quinn's disdain.

Madelyn had rushed into the coffee shop, waving at the two of them enthusiastically, and was ordering at the front kiosk. Her glasses fogged from the November chill outside, but she'd kept them on, letting them slide down her nose so she could look at the world above them. A massively overloaded backpack slumped to the side of Madelyn's right leg, where she'd dumped it upon arriving at the till.

"How old is she, again?" asked Quinn.

"I know she looks young, but we're the same age. She's just short."

"And dorky," added Quinn.

"Since when is that a crime?"

Quinn pulled her hand back a bit, but Georgie held on. "I was expecting different from the way you talked about her."

"How did I talk about her?"

"I don't know," said Quinn. She surveyed Georgie coolly. Whatever Georgie had done, apparently it had been wrong. "You made her sound like such a badass."

"She is, in her own way. Try fighting against her in a model U.N. debate." Georgie snorted with laughter at the memory.

"Mmm," said Quinn. She sipped her coffee, foot bouncing.

Madelyn took a mug from the barista and made her way over, scarf unravelling from her neck so that it draped ominously close to the coffee. Just before disaster struck, she dropped into the free chair at Quinn and Georgie's table.

"Sorry I'm late!" Madelyn said, brightly. "I'm Madelyn."

Though Madelyn held out a hand to shake with Quinn, there was a moment where it appeared that Quinn wasn't going to extend her own. That hesitation struck a vivid panic into Georgie's nerves, her skin crawling with dread. But the moment passed, and the two shook hands.

They'd met, and the world hadn't stopped rotating on its axis.

Could Georgie maybe get over herself for a second, now?

She wasn't sure why she'd been so apprehensive. Madelyn launched into a barrage of questions about Quinn's course schedule, assignments, part-time work clientele, and more. Her innate curiosity about people had always charmed Georgie. She hoped it would do the same with her new girlfriend.

"It's just a youth center," Quinn said, shrugging.

"But that's amazing! You're doing everything you can to make the world a better place. Queer students must be so happy that you do your work," Madelyn said. She cradled her mug in both hands and her attention was riveted onto Quinn's every micro-expression.

"I guess I do what I can, yeah."

Why wasn't Quinn filling in the gap in conversation with questions about Madelyn?

A pause sat heavily while Madelyn sipped her coffee. Apparently refreshed, she continued.

"So do you have siblings? Wait—let me guess! You're the middle child."

"Oldest, actually."

"Interesting. You have more of a middle vibe." Madelyn smiled, but Quinn didn't.

"Like, forgettable?"

Georgie's smile felt strained, and she was sure it didn't reach her eyes, but she interjected regardless. "I'm sure that's not what Madelyn meant."

"Of course not," added Madelyn. The speck of foam on her upper lip distracted Georgie for just long enough that she didn't attempt to persuade Quinn further.

"Ok, fine," said Quinn. She didn't outright huff, but Georgie sensed the frustration under the surface. This was going nowhere near as well as she'd hoped. Still, there was plenty of time left to help them connect.

"Quinn's younger brother is a gymnast," she offered. A tidbit of information, just enough to smooth things over.

"Cool! I always wished I could learn to do backflips," Madelyn said. "Remember that time we went to the foam pit for Grade 5 gym class, Georgie? I barely went in, I was so scared."

Georgie laughed at the memory. "Yeah and I dove in first, before Mrs. Dzidyk was even done explaining the rules."

"Typical," said Madelyn. Her eyes shone with amusement, so much so that Georgie's gaze stayed there a second too long. Madelyn's sandy hair framed her face in loose waves, her cold-reddened cheeks perfectly fresh and bright. Georgie's lingering attention made her heart rush despite herself.

"Did you ever try lessons?" asked Quinn. Finally, a question. Too bad it was loaded with a biting tone.

"For... the foam pit?" As always, Madelyn's confusion manifested as her tilting her head and biting her lip. She wore her emotions on her face so readily, like filtering herself for the world was impossible. Georgie bit her own lip while she watched Madelyn.

"No, backflips. You didn't try to learn?"

"I think Madelyn just meant it was a cool thing to be able to do," Georgie said.

This was hard as hell.

If Georgie had known how much Quinn and Madelyn's personalities would clash, she might've made much simpler plans. Saying hello after class or something.

"My brother trains for hours a day. It's a huge commitment and we're really proud of him," Quinn said.

"Yeah, I wouldn't really have time for that kind of thing these days. Too many awesome classes to take!" Madelyn said, nodding. She waited, apparently to see if Quinn would expand on what she'd said earlier, but no more conversation seemed forthcoming.

Georgie wasn't sure how to get through the rest of the hour before she and Quinn had to leave for class. Juggling had never been her strong suit, and right now Madelyn and Quinn were so imbalanced that the only thing keeping them from falling completely apart was Georgie's wide-eyed insistence on their having something in common.

It hadn't occurred to Georgie that the thing in common might be her attention.

When Madelyn finished her coffee and checked her phone, she'd gotten a text from a group project member about some last-minute changes they needed to do. Georgie mentally breathed a sigh of relief. She couldn't do another ten minutes of this, let alone forty.

She and Quinn sat in silence while Madelyn packed up and left, waving happily back at them and continuing to say how nice it was to see each other, despite the way it disrupted the coffee shop patrons along her path to the exit. Her smile was cheerful as ever.

"Did you have to be so difficult with her?" Georgie asked Quinn, but Quinn's instantly furrowed brow told her she'd spoken without thinking.

"Me difficult? She's the one who wouldn't let me get a word in. Too focused on how you two have been friends forever, like so close and so perfect and everything, to even want to really know me."

"That's not true, Quinn. She was so curious about you. She tried to get to know you."

"More like in love with the sound of her own voice. No wonder she wants to be a professor—standing in front of a captive audience sounds exactly her style."

"She loves history so much. I don't think you're being fair."

Quinn looked for a second like she'd been slapped, and then she composed herself with steely resolve. "No, Georgie, I don't think you are. I'm going to go, and when you've gotten over your reflexive need to defend your best friend over me, give me a call."

As she watched Quinn stride out of the coffee shop, Georgie fumed. She was furious with Quinn for being so unwilling to see the good in Madelyn, angry at Madelyn for bubbling over with enthusiasm so much so that she didn't think about how serious this was for Georgie, and most of all, frustrated with herself. Because she'd told Quinn she used to have a crush on Madelyn, and now that seemed to be the only thing Quinn had considered.

She dawdled her whole way back to campus, not wanting to see anyone she knew.

That evening, Georgie's phone buzzed. Maybe it was Quinn apologizing for her abrupt, selfish exit to their date.

Nope.

Madelyn: "Awesome to meet Quinn today! Can I call you in a few?"

Georgie didn't bother to wait. She dialed Madelyn's number right away in response.

"Hey," said Madelyn.

"Hey," said Georgie. "So, uh, sorry about that."

"Oh my god, Georgie, it's not your fault! I'm so glad you introduced me to her. Like, your first girlfriend. That's a big deal. I just wanted to see how you felt about it."

"Not good, Mads."

"Yeah..."

The pause felt so much better than that of the coffee shop earlier today. Silence with Madelyn wasn't just tolerable, it was comfortable.

"I thought she'd have been nicer to you. I really am sorry."

"No, no, no. It's ok. Honestly, Georgie. She's really pretty, by the way!"

And that had indeed been what drew Georgie to Quinn in the first place: her long, sleek brown hair that looked like she'd always emerged recently from a professional blow-out salon. The firm, perky fullness of the breasts that Quinn actually wanted Georgie to touch. It had seemed too good to be true.

Maybe it was.

"Pretty, yeah. Thanks."

"What else? Umm. She's clearly super into you, which is so nice to see. You deserve to be with someone who feels that way about you."

"Thanks, Mads," said Georgie. She didn't feel thankful, though. Her guts were still twisted with anger and anguish. "But I wanted her to like you."

"She will, don't worry about me. I think I just overwhelmed her with my questions. I know I can be a lot to handle at first, and we'll have so much time to get to know each other better while you keep dating. Unless... do you still want to date her?"

Another pause while Georgie deliberated. "I don't know. She was rude to you, and that's not ok with me."

"Maybe we just need to meet on more neutral ground. Without you to chaperone, we could really talk. Get past this initial hurdle."

But Georgie could picture how that would make Quinn accuse her of throwing her to the wolves, of not caring enough to support her through getting to know Madelyn. She was damned the one way, and the other.

"I don't think that's a good idea. And it's not your fault, Mads. Quinn's being unreasonable."

"Ugh. I'm sorry to hear that."

"Honestly, I'm surprised. We've been going out long enough I didn't think she'd be insecure. She was so jealous."

"Jealous? Of me?"

Shit. Georgie forgot what she'd been saying and accidentally let things slip that she'd worked excruciatingly hard to conceal.

"You know, we're best friends, and she doesn't like that there's another woman in my life whose history with me outweighs hers. And always will."

"Aw, that's kind of sweet except the part where she's being irrational and unfair."

"Ha, exactly."

"Well, I liked her. Even if she didn't like me all that much."

"You're too sweet, but thanks." Georgie's gut surged with affection for Madelyn. No matter what happened, she could always count on her best friend to rise above petty drama. She was, as they said, a keeper.

Too bad she was straight and therefore highly unlikely to want to be kept by Georgie. Let alone any other woman.

Angst glimmered in Georgie's blood about this, her time-worn hobby horse. You could wait for someone to love you, sure, if there was a shot in hell. But short of a seriously invasive brainwashing session, Madelyn was completely unattainable.

"Is Quinn always so insecure?" asked Madelyn. Her question arose from innocent curiosity; Georgie knew her well enough to understand that. But the way it skirted near Georgie's deepest secrets brought her hackles up.

She couldn't say what she really wanted to—couldn't spill every messy feeling into the phone and have Madelyn pick each one up. Not without breaking the trust they had and severing parts of the friendship forever. Not without confronting the fact Georgie was holding out for the impossible.

If you never risked saying the truth, you could pretend. Could grasp the last shreds of your dignity and tell yourself they were still yours and not co-opted by emotions you couldn't control.

"Not usually, no," said Georgie. She breathed steadily, counting for a few beats so that the answer wouldn't rush out of her and sound rehearsed. Still, she knew she wasn't being entirely honest. "Like I said, she seems especially insecure about things with you. I can't promise I did my best to quell those fears, but you know me. I can be stubborn."

Especially about you, thought Georgie. Words she could never speak.

"Fucking rights you can be!" laughed Madelyn. "Quinn's got another think coming if she's convinced you'll just let her blast insecurity everywhere without you fighting it."

That voice on the phone with her was so accepting of what Georgie said when she needed support, so measured in thoughtful critique when she was being an ass. Madelyn had oceans more depth than Quinn.

How could Georgie not have seen it until now?

She had to have been kidding herself. Horny and desperate enough to jump at the first girlfriend opportunity that came her way, hoping it would erase the deeper feelings she concealed.

Of course, it didn't.

"The thing is, Mads, I don't know if I want to fight it. I shouldn't be having a fight like this at all. Girlfriends are supposed to accept who you are. And part of who I am is friends with you. A big part."

"That's part of me, too, G. You don't think she'd come around?"

Georgie wanted to believe Quinn could. But this conflict had revealed something more unsettling and difficult to digest. And that was that Georgie wasn't as over Madelyn as she'd thought she was. Maybe not at all.

The moment Quinn had essentially forced her to choose sides, it hadn't even been a contest. Whoever did that automatically became the loser, in Georgie's view. And if they were up against Madelyn?

They'd always, always come second.

15

Present Day

Madelyn left the cabin early, having talked her heart out with Nadia and Hannah. She'd longed to have time to do the same with Georgie, but since Georgie left and texts wouldn't send in this service deadzone, Madelyn would have to wait.

And just like that, Madelyn's best chance at happiness seemed to have evaporated as quickly as the steam above the spa hot tubs in the town of Banff. She watched the droves of tourists snapping mountain pictures and posing in front of Canadian stores like Roots, but the green light changed and the person behind her honked.

Time to go home.

It would have been easier if Madelyn knew what she was doing. Instead of certainty, instead of airing her feelings and maybe sparking the start of something truly life-changing, everything had gone wrong. She'd told Georgie about her feelings in the stupidest way possible.

That was already catastrophic.

Then she'd hurt herself, necessitating a visit to the Mediclinic when she got home so she could make sure there wasn't a fracture somewhere in her swollen ankle. A tensor bandage might help fix her injury, but there wasn't a surface fix available for her deeply bruised ego.

In a cabin with no other distractions, with the power out and the snowstorm raging, Georgie still hadn't given Madelyn her full attention. And the only explanation Madelyn could find for that was that Georgie didn't feel the same way as her.

Sometimes friendship was just that, and nothing more.

But what about the fact their closest friends saw something? Nadia and Hannah had thought Georgie carried a torch for Madelyn. When Georgie moved away, had the torch gone out?

Madelyn didn't know what to think. She cranked her saddest-sack music on the drive back to Calgary, watching the mountains roll down into foothills, become undulating prairie, morph into grassy plains dotted with suburban homes and strip malls.

When the landscape had lulled her into a sense of peaceful return, Madelyn's eye was caught by a blur of brown motion to her right. A deer ran alongside the highway, its white hindquarters the only thing that stood out from the brushy ditch. Madelyn wondered, for a split second, where it was going.

And then she remembered that where one deer can be found, there are often others. Too late, she slammed the brakes on her car. The momentum carried her forwards so quickly that she could do nothing but pray when another deer, larger than the first, hopped onto the pavement directly in front of her.

A sickening shuddering feeling rocked the car as Madelyn braked. Traffic wasn't bad, so no one was behind her.

Just in time, she stopped.

She tried to calm her racing heart while she stared out the windshield at the deer. It blinked placidly and sauntered across the rest of the pavement over to the ditch on the other side. Meanwhile, Madelyn's pulse pounded and her hands shook on the steering wheel.

Pull over. Calm down.

Underneath the whispers of logic, Madelyn saw flashes of the snow-covered fawn in the woods. She drove to the shoulder and put her car in park before bursting into tears.

With her heart still racing, she took out her phone and texted Georgie.

"Almost hit a deer. I'm so scared. What do you do if you hit one, again?"

Just before she pressed send, she remembered the last week. It had completely slipped her mind in the urgency of a crisis. Her first instinct had been that Georgie could fix everything.

Georgie *would* fix everything. That was who she was—strong, capable, giving.

Rather than crying at the side of the road like Madelyn, Georgie would stay calm. At that thought, Madelyn sobbed even harder. Here she was, miserable over nearly killing an innocent animal, and the most upsetting part was that her friend wasn't there to help her. She'd ruined that, too.

She deleted the text. It felt wrong, but not much felt right in Madelyn's life right then, anyway.

What was one more close call along the way?

Finally, she calmed down enough to wipe the tears from her face and get back onto the highway. Without turning her music back on, she drove home. It took less time than she thought it would, since her mind was preoccupied.

At home, Madelyn emerged from her car into the city

air, listening to the surprising volume of tires on pavement. The honking, beeping, bustling city noise was so obvious compared to the silence at the cabin. Her apartment wasn't much, but it was supposed to be home.

Today, though, it felt like a holding cell. Her punishment for messing things up badly with Georgie and ruining her future.

Hold up, Madelyn. Who's to say she'd have wanted to be with you even if you did have a chance?

Madelyn had been presumptuous from the start. Her elation at discovering she loved Georgie had assumed that it would be matched with something similar. That telling Georgie her feelings would be a form of catharsis, of healing.

She hadn't considered how Georgie might feel to be trapped with that confession. How maybe Georgie had had a crush a long time ago and worked hard to get past it.

God, she'd been stupid.

It took an astonishing amount of effort to close the flimsy Wal-Mart blinds to Madelyn's bedroom window. She rolled into bed exhausted and melted into tears, letting them fall without even trying to keep them in.

Finally, she could wallow. A good, deep crying session left her spent and shaky, but by the time the darkness of the night sank her apartment into shadows, Madelyn felt she'd exorcised something all-consuming.

What would be left was still to be determined. She checked her phone, hoping against logic that Georgie would have reached out and confessed her own feelings, apologized for leaving suddenly, and offered to make new plans to live in Calgary again. Though Madelyn knew these wishes were fantastical, she felt them anyway.

It would be up to her to fix things, that was clear. And

leaving them broken was not an option, not after twenty years of knowing each other. If Madelyn didn't know Georgie, she wasn't sure that being alive was even worth it. The thought was unbearable.

She called Georgie, letting the phone ring as long as it needed to get to the voicemail. She hadn't expected Georgie to answer but sadness surged in her all the same when the robotic voice welcomed her to the voicemail inbox.

"Georgie," said Madelyn. "We've known each other for so long, and have so much history together, that I don't really know where to start. Just know that I realize I messed things up this week. And I want to make it up to you, if I can. Losing your friendship would be the only thing I can't stand right now, even if the sun started making its way to destroy the planet, I'd still want to choose you. Not that I could fix the apocalypse, but you know what I mean. Or maybe you don't. Anyway, please take as much time as you need, if that's what you need. I'll be here, I promise. No expectations."

She'd gotten so hung up on wanting a romantic relationship that she'd forgotten that risking their friendship was a dumb, dumb move. It would be better to have platonic Georgie, a thousand times over, than no Georgie in her life at all.

So Madelyn set herself to the task of sifting through her belongings, one by one, and finding all the evidence she could of her lifelong friendship with Georgie. She needed to remind herself of the depth and value of that bond, and maybe Georgie could use it too. Madelyn suspected so, and that was a risk she could manage. The Mediclinic could wait until tomorrow.

"Look at this kindergarten class photo, G. Your hair was so cute back then. Think you'll get back into doing your own haircuts? :)" She texted Georgie a picture of the photograph, affection tightening her chest.

Madelyn found a box of handwritten notes to one another from elementary school underneath her stack of grade-school photos. In each note, Madelyn had signed a fancy faux-script M as if she were a princess in training, while Georgie had just written her initials in block letters. They talked about Pokémon, television shows, what other kids in the room were doing that they found annoying. The smile on Madelyn's face overshadowed her urge to cry.

"Look how much we used to talk. I can't believe I used to be this pretentious about my signature!" she captioned the next photo she sent Georgie, of a note where Madelyn complained about not getting 100% on a recent spelling test and then signed her full name in the 'font' she'd been using in all her other notes.

It didn't matter to Madelyn that Georgie wasn't responding to her texts yet. The receipts still showed that the messages were delivered and not yet read. What was important was that she was rediscovering, intentionally, what had bound them together in the first place. Reminding herself of their value as a team. Maybe, just maybe, helping Georgie feel less alone.

If that was what it took, she would comb through every last scrap of paper from their childhood and adolescence.

Next, Madelyn found the dog-eared and worn copy of a pulpy noir detective novel, *Silent Gamine*, Georgie had bought in a garage sale during middle school. That book had quickly become one of their favorites. They had taken turns reading it out loud to each other and trying to parse the meaning of certain euphemistic turns of phrase that didn't outlast the 1940s.

"Remember 'gams' and our obsession with this book?"

Madelyn wrote, the tears now fully dried on her face and replaced by a warm smile. She was grateful she never threw anything out, now, because it was providing her with exactly the kind of solace she needed.

Pictures of Halloween costumes, digital files with recordings of them pretending to host news talk shows, badly written essays on the virtues of actresses they loved that had since languished in obscurity—the whole lot of Madelyn's friendship with Georgie shone with their closeness. It had barely been possible to spend a day without seeing each other or at least calling, texting, or sending instant messages over MSN.

Madelyn had known she was upset over Georgie's move to Edmonton, had since felt shame for how she'd treated it like a crushing blow when she should have showed Georgie excitement and support. But she had failed to understand where that anguish had come from.

Of course, part of it was her unacknowledged feelings. A larger portion, yet to be explained to Georgie, was how they'd gone from 0 to 100, in reverse. Constant contact, support, and laughter had been replaced with infrequent texts and monthly Skype calls.

And during those calls, Georgie often said little. She was normally reserved even around Madelyn, but the distance altered that silence from bearable to stony. All the warmth had drained from their interactions.

She had sent screenshots of a few threads from when Georgie and Madelyn binge-watched Orange is the New Black together while texting reaction GIFs back and forth. In this light, she saw how even then, she'd been flirting with Georgie—without realizing it. One message read "Ruby Rose is STUNNING" and had a cartoon with heart-eyes in it. A few hours later, she'd written that Ruby reminded her of Georgie.

"I miss us," texted Madelyn. She'd sent photos of so many memories, she was worried Georgie might think she'd gone insane. But this last message, she knew she had to send. It was the crux of all her sadness, the pain that she couldn't dislodge, no matter how much she reviewed their lives so far. Once it left her phone and sped through the ether to Georgie, Madelyn was able to breathe again.

No matter what came of this, she'd done what she needed to do.

Shortly afterwards, like her body had been running on fumes for the last few hours, Madelyn fell into a deep, surprisingly restful sleep. Though she dreamed of nothing, it was the good kind of nothing. A soothing darkness completely enveloped her, leaving no space for the pain and sorrows of her wakeful day.

In the morning, she would try calling Georgie again.

16

Age 24

Georgie hadn't expected Madelyn's call, but it hadn't been unwelcome, either. The late-night hour wasn't unusual; the two talked so frequently that it was an unspoken understanding that no matter the time, you could send a message. It might not be seen until later, but communication was always an option.

Even so, there was an odd structure to Madelyn's speech that made Georgie anxious.

Was she having a breakdown?

Typically, Madelyn wasn't terse. Far from it. Thoughts poured from her like a waterfall, sometimes splashing around all over before Georgie could form a single sentence. Tonight, though, Madelyn's breath had been strained and her words mumbled.

"Come over," Georgie had said. Crisis took precedence over sleep. Madelyn was a priority, and if she needed help, Georgie was more than willing to give it. In whatever shape it took.

She cleared empty energy drink bottles from the desk,

stuck a few dirty dishes into the dishwasher that had been lying around. Just as the buzzer rang, Georgie shoved a vibrator under the bed.

She let Madelyn in and sat at the small table in her kitchen waiting for her to make her way up the flights of stairs. No elevator for this cheap building, not that Georgie minded. Helped keep her humble and in shape. She enjoyed the flexing feeling that came from her quads after making the trip up. The exhaustion in her arms from carrying groceries, piled several bags deep on each side.

When Madelyn knocked, the sound was so quiet that Georgie almost missed it.

"Hey," she said, opening the door. "What's up?"

One glance at Madelyn's red eyes and Georgie knew this wasn't a trip she'd taken lightly. Madelyn had been crying for a long time. Without asking more, Georgie went to her fridge and got a beer for Madelyn, cracking it with the magnetic opener shaped like a longhorn bull.

"Thank you," said Madelyn. Her words shook, vibrating with sadness. Georgie ushered her into the living room and guided her to the couch. So many nights had been spent watching Jeopardy here, talking about life and plans and wondering where the future might take them. Georgie had lived in this dump for five years now.

It was only six blocks away from Madelyn's apartment.

"Do I need to punch a guy? Mark hurt you?" ventured Georgie.

Normally the tough-as-nails bravado made Madelyn laugh, but she exhaled with a ragged, sad noise. "No, no. Nothing like that." Georgie's gut screamed for her to hug her, hold her.

"Good. Cause I'd pulverize him. I think he knows that, too."

Madelyn's weak smile faltered as soon as it appeared on her face.

The silence that followed ached with so many feelings, Georgie found herself clearing her throat to make it stop hurting. Her eyes prickled with the threat of tears; the sight of Madelyn so devastated was unbelievably painful.

"Mads?"

Madelyn sighed, deeply, and scratched at the label of the beer bottle. Her chipped nail polish made Georgie warm internally at the way Madelyn's ever-the-whirlwind life showed up in small details.

"Mark and I broke up," she said. Madelyn's voice intoned the last part of the sentence with a rising sound, as if she were asking Georgie whether it had happened rather than telling her. But the truth remained.

Small, staccato heartbeats echoed in Georgie's chest, more noticeable than before Madelyn spoke. It was irrational, she knew that. But Madelyn and Mark had been together for years now. She hated to see her friend sad, of course, but the deep-seated emotional core of Georgie also secretly rejoiced.

"I'm sorry," she said. It wasn't enough, and she knew it. But how could she fully express that she didn't want Madelyn to hurt, and yet also didn't think Mark was good enough for her?

No man was.

Somehow, they never saw Madelyn the right way, the way where her light shone brightly because of some internal compass, not something that existed just for them. Madelyn's boyfriends were always too willing to experience her, not eager enough to reciprocate her joy.

She deserved so much more. Maybe now, finally, Madelyn could have a chance at the expansive, all-consuming love she yearned for. Georgie sat, armpits hinting nervous sweat, wishing she didn't want to be that all-consuming love. She felt it anyway.

"That's part of it," Madelyn said. Her voice was practically a whisper. It drew Georgie closer and she found her breath hitching at the proximity. From here, she could see the delicate movements of Madelyn's throat as she swallowed a sip of beer. Could watch Madelyn's heartbeat in that soft, smooth skin.

Snap out of it, Georgie. Your friend needs help, not lust.

"What else is going on?" Georgie said. It seemed obvious to her that her voice was strangled with feeling, but Madelyn didn't look up. Didn't flinch.

"Georgie," said Madelyn, turning her head to look Georgie straight in the eye. It was arresting, as it always was: the clarity of her pupils, startling and stunning. Lips curved like she was about to whistle. Cheeks stained with since-dried tears and flushed with half-dissipated feeling.

"Yeah?"

"Promise you won't judge me?"

Georgie had never taken any promise more seriously. "Of course not. Want to pinky swear?"

Madelyn smiled, a small, faltering smile. It was brighter than the sun to Georgie. "No, I'm good. I just..."

This silence was warmer. Though Madelyn's pain still shone from her curled-up posture, the mere act of being together seemed to ease the worst of it. Georgie pulled her feet underneath herself and tried to remember active listening skills.

"Anything you tell me, I will always, always care. No judgments here. Right? We've known each other too long. Too well."

"Thanks," said Madelyn. She smiled down at her beer bottle and then drank a bigger gulp. "So I think I'm gay."

Stars burst in Georgie's eyes and she felt a whine begin deep in the lowest part of her skull. The pin-prick hint of sweat beneath her arms began to trickle. "What?"

It was such an inadequate thing to say.

'What?'—like she hadn't heard.

Hadn't fantasized about this very moment for how long?

And now Georgie was paralyzed, unable to help her friend because her mind had begun to race, her body was thrown into an immediate frenzy of desperate, self-centered hope. While she should have been focused on how to be supportive, Georgie's long-held crush reared its head.

"Like, I like girls? Not boys. Or more than boys, I'm not sure. Maybe I won't ever know for certain, but what I do know is I don't love Mark. Or, I love him, but I'm not in love with him."

"That's... a lot." Georgie stared at Madelyn, and when she realized she'd been staring, she flushed beet red and redirected her gaze to her own hands. They were a little pink, too. Like every part of her was overloaded with blood, racing around completely maniacally from this shock.

Welcome though it might be, it was still a shock.

"I know. And I don't know what to do. This is, like, shit you're supposed to figure out in high school, right? You've always known so clearly who you are and what you want. Why can't I have that?"

Madelyn's voice faltered and tears sprang to her eyes, spilling readily down those soft cheeks.

"It's ok to be upset," said Georgie.

"I don't want to be, though."

"Right. But even if you're upset, you should know something. Maybe it looked easy on the outside, to you, but for me, coming out wasn't obvious. So don't beat yourself up about it."

"Really?"

"Yeah. Don't you remember how terrified I was?"

"You always look so cool, no matter what you're doing."

Georgie laughed and didn't fight the puff of pride she felt hearing that compliment. It came from such a lovely source.

"Maybe I looked like I wasn't panicked, but I swear to you that I was. It felt like my world was ending, and I'd lose everything I cared about."

"I do care about Mark, that's part of what sucks about this."

Georgie shuffled closer on the couch, resting a hand on Madelyn's forearm. "You do. Living together and sharing a life together still means something. But caring about him and being in love with him can be separate things. And if you care about him, it makes sense not to stay together if you don't love him that way."

"Is it terrible if part of why I broke up with him was to start dating again, though? I want to see what my life could be like, you know, honestly."

Laughter burst out of Georgie. "If you're looking to get shit for wanting to date girls, you've come to the wrong place."

Madelyn sighed again. "No, this is exactly where I needed to be. Thanks Georgie."

In between each sentence, Georgie tried to walk back from the dizzying ledge she'd come to in her mind. If there had been any sign whatsoever that Madelyn felt romantically inclined towards her, Georgie would have thrown herself into it. She'd worked hard to repress her feelings for Madelyn only to have her run over and give her a sign.

Hope didn't have to mean delusion.

There had never been a better chance for them than now.

Georgie knew she was thinking unrealistically. But her heart didn't care.

"And don't think you need to have it all figured out. You've got time. I mean, for fuck's sake, you're only 24. Don't act like your life is over. There's plenty of time for dating."

With a final swig, Madelyn finished her beer and set it on the coffee table next to Georgie's stacks of half-read comic books. "You're right. So much time. It'll take some time to get over Mark, but I can throw myself into my research in the meantime. Set my Tinder up again and change the settings. When I say that out loud it actually sounds super fun."

"Don't rush, though," said Georgie. Her words appeared to be in vain, because Madelyn took her phone out and opened the App store.

"I swear to god, I think I've forgotten every password I've ever created."

Panic rose in Georgie's gut, watching Madelyn sign into Tinder and change her preferences to women. It was too soon, too late at night. Too focused on something shallow and meaningless when she should have been getting the logistics sorted of where she'd live if she wouldn't be with Mark.

Underneath those rational concerns, Georgie also felt snubbed. Of all the queer women Madelyn knew, shouldn't she be turning to Georgie for advice the most? For a night on the town, a chance at meeting people in real life, or maybe... noticing there was someone right there who'd been there all along.

"It's getting late," Georgie said quietly. She rubbed Madelyn's shoulder to bring her out of her excitement.

"Guess so. Oh man, this is going to be fun! Look at her," said Madelyn. She showed her phone to Georgie, revealing a picture of some femme-y blonde with a nose ring and cat eye liner that was so sharp it could cut flesh. "Do you think she'd like me?"

Georgie didn't want to be doing this. Her ears might have stopped ringing, but now a new, internal alarm was going off. It was wrong. It was all wrong, and Madelyn didn't see how wrong it was.

"Anyone who doesn't like you isn't worth your time," she said. Trying to keep the emotion out of her voice, fighting to rein in the way her heart longed for her to spill everything, right now. Lay it on the table and make the case for herself as a candidate.

"Technically true, but I was looking for something more like 'Of course! You're so cute anyone would like you!'" Madelyn said, batting her eyelashes playfully at Georgie. The resulting hammering in Georgie's chest distracted her from her goals.

"Madelyn, you're stunning. And you're a beautiful person underneath the surface, too. When you're ready to date, you'll be a catch."

"Why thank you!" cooed Madelyn, batting at Georgie's arm flirtatiously. She laughed and then came closer, each step making Georgie short circuit just a little more.

This wasn't happening.

Not like this.

She couldn't be Madelyn's rebound. Touching her, getting to be part of her life in that way would be incredible, but Georgie was in it for the long haul. The real shit.

"Uh, Mads—" she said, trying her best to politely rebuff the flirtation, stiffening her posture and raising an eyebrow.

"Oh, don't worry, Georgie. I'm joking—I would never date you!"

It spilled out of Madelyn's mouth so easily. Such harmful words spoken so sweetly, so lightly. Georgie fought the urge to gasp and double over in pain.

"Mm," she mumbled, all her energy now focused on preserving essential functions. She could barely breathe, let alone speak English.

Never!

Never?

Never.

Georgie had thought she'd been through every emotion that Madelyn could prompt in her already. She'd thought the lows she'd experienced were over, a high school remnant of pain long since processed and filed away under 'coming of age queer in a straight-majority environment.'

Nothing could have prepared her for this.

"I'll figure it out," Madelyn murmured to herself. If Georgie wasn't mistaken, she sounded tipsy. Maybe she'd had something to drink before coming over. Maybe that beer had been the final piece of a heartbroken puzzle.

Maybe none of that fucking mattered, because what Madelyn had just said cut worse than anything Georgie could have expected to hear from her, ever.

There was no better way to devastate Georgie.

"I think it's time for bed," Georgie managed to say, her eyes unable to meet Madelyn's.

Whatever Madelyn said in response, it didn't reach Georgie's brain, which still whirred with the obsessive, self-harming focus on how Madelyn had so casually destroyed Georgie's longest running hope, misguided as it may have been.

She set up the couch with a pillow and blankets and

then steered Madelyn to the bedroom.

"I couldn't! That's your bed. I'll take the couch," she protested, but when Georgie turned and walked away, it must have been enough to finalize the matter. Georgie sank onto the couch and slept fitfully, her every dream poisoned by having reality slapped squarely across her face.

She had spent a lifetime waiting around for Madelyn to be who Georgie wanted her to be, but no amount of insane self-deception could justify waiting any more. If Madelyn was queer and still didn't want Georgie, it was time for a change.

Georgie couldn't do this anymore, and when she woke in the morning, it was clear that she needed space. Real, enforced space. Something that would require her to stop talking to Madelyn so much, to stop expecting so much from her, when her feelings were obviously never going to be reciprocated.

It was time for Georgie to get over her.

A few weeks later, Georgie's sister Ariel helped load the contents of her sparsely furnished apartment into her beaten-up pickup truck. Rather than face the friends who knew Madelyn and Georgie both, Georgie found herself wishing for familial comfort, support from a person who was more clearly on her side.

With the packages loaded onto the back of her truck, Georgie closed the tailgate and turned to her sister.

"Thanks for showing up for me, Ariel," she said. Tears wavered on the brink of spilling, surprising Georgie and Ariel both.

"Take care of yourself, Georgie," said Ariel. She drew Georgie into an affectionate hug, and Georgie let herself cry onto the soft pink sweater, knowing that all forms of comfort would soon seem very far away indeed.

17

Present Day

Madelyn's phone history now showed call after outgoing call to Georgie. None where Georgie picked up, but Madelyn was still hopeful. With all the text messages she'd sent Georgie's way, there was nothing more Madelyn could do except wait.

First, she waited at the Mediclinic, where they informed her, after a couple hours and several x-rays, that she'd merely sprained her ankle and ought to rest it. Then she went home and sat in front of her phone, willing it to buzz with Georgie's response. When none came, Madelyn threw herself into distraction.

She took the opportunity to finally work on the revisions to her paper. Better late than never. It had seemed before like there were so many that she'd never finish them, but with a full night's sleep and the exercise of going through Georgie memories under her belt, Madelyn felt more optimistic than she had in weeks, maybe months.

Madelyn addressed one comment at a time, starting with the easiest suggestion. This reviewer preferred British spelling for several of the words Madelyn had unwittingly Americanized. That was simple to find and replace. With a little more confidence built having completed those edits, Madelyn tucked into the more substantive critiques.

Before long, her paper began to look much better. At least, she thought so. Albertan women's wartime contributions would now have a new voice. But working made Madelyn hungry, so she ordered a pizza and chopped carrot sticks in the meantime.

When the buzzer went off, Madelyn's stomach growled in anticipation and she let the delivery guy in. Soon, a firm hand knocked at her apartment door. When she opened the door, debit card in hand, she jumped.

"Georgie?"

She stood there, pizza box in hand and a sheepish expression on her face. The denim jacket over her old high school t-shirt fit in a way that emphasized her shoulders, and she slouched to one side, hip extended, like she might run off instead of staying until Madelyn found words to speak.

"Hey, uh. Ran into the pizza guy on the way here and I paid for it instead."

"Thanks. Oh my god. Come in," Madelyn said. She was shaking from surprise and perhaps a little anxiety. "Did you drive here today? I've been calling you."

"I know," said Georgie. She put the pizza down and sat on the footstool near Madelyn's desk. "I wasn't ready to talk yet."

"But you were ok with driving for hours without even checking if I was home?"

"Let's be real, Madelyn. I knew you'd either be here or the library."

Madelyn laughed despite herself and then frowned as if

retaliating against her own renegade feelings. "I could have been staying with my parents, or friends."

"Nope. Checked with everyone. Not that that was easy, mind you."

"I thought you were mad at Hannah and Nadia?"

Georgie sighed and grabbed a slice of pizza out of the box. "Yeah. I said a bunch of nasty things to them in my head on the drive home from Banff. But it turns out the person I was the angriest at was myself."

"Deep," said Madelyn, winking at Georgie, who wasn't normally the kind of person to speak like this.

"I'm serious, Mads."

Madelyn stopped smiling and tried, instead, to focus on Georgie with her every breath. This was important.

"It's fucking embarrassing to think that everyone talked about how I was into you. If they'd had a bet going, thought we'd hook up or end up together, it drove me crazy. I owe you an apology because I didn't mean to storm out like that, but by the time I cooled down I was hours away on a shitty highway. Icy."

"I'm glad you didn't risk your life to come back. With me, it can wait. You know that, right? It can always wait. I'm here and I'm not going anywhere." Madelyn moved so that she could sit next to Georgie. The radiant energy of Georgie's body pulled her closer. Barring their time at the cabin, it had been almost a year since they'd been able to be in the same room.

It felt good.

"You say that now, but I've spent years convinced that if you knew how I felt about you, you'd run. It never occurred to me that everyone in our friend circle could tell that was how I felt. Fuckin' sucks, you know? You think you're guarding this precious secret and then they all laugh about it the moment it's out."

"I didn't laugh," said Madelyn.

"I know," Georgie sighed. "Thanks for that."

A moment passed. Madelyn wasn't sure where to dig in, but Georgie began talking again.

"I have loved you since as long as I've known how to love, Madelyn. Longer than I was aware of, longer than any relationship I've had with any girlfriend. That's scary as fuck."

Madelyn's stomach tightened and quivered at Georgie's words; she had prepared herself for the absolute worst yesterday, that their friendship would be over and done with. Nothing could have made Madelyn ready for this.

"I love you, too, Georgie."

"But here's the thing:"

In Georgie's inhalation, Madelyn saw flashes of disaster, impending doom sure to shatter their relationship before it began. Her mind worked overtime in assuming negative outcomes.

Georgie had been using the past tense, hadn't she?

"Hm?"

"You really hurt me," said Georgie.

There it was—the beginning of the end. Georgie had come down here to break up with her as a friend and as a lover. It was decent of her to make the trip, but Madelyn had let herself calm down too soon. She wasn't ready for this kind of heartbreak.

How could she ever be?

"I'm sorry," Madelyn said through the tears that sprang up instantly. They streamed freely, tracing paths down her cheeks that she did nothing to stop. "Georgie, I'm sorry."

"Please just listen."

"Ok." The noise from the street outside buzzed deep in Madelyn's brain.

"Do you remember when you came over to my place last year? Before I moved to Edmonton?"

Madelyn nodded, still crying. The night Georgie had been there for her, no questions asked. She'd needed support and Georgie had given it.

"When you said that you'd never see me that way, something inside me broke. All those years of pining and you could just callously joke about me your first day of being out. I knew I needed space. To get over you."

Gravity suddenly felt three times as powerful, and Madelyn sank into herself. "Wait, no. So you're over..."

"That's why I moved. I know I said the job opportunity was too good to pass up, but it was a lie. I needed room. Time. To find some closure on that stupid dream I had that you might see me that way."

“So it's all done?”

A siren somewhere in the distance blared. Madelyn's shoulders shook with emotion and she cried out of frustration now as well as heartbreak.

"That cut me deep. And when the rest of the group walked in on us... together, I didn't think I could ever get over that, either. You know me, I hate feelings. Would rather not have any, to be completely honest."

"Ok, I can accept what you're saying, but stop for a second," Madelyn said. The anger in her voice gave Georgie pause long enough for Madelyn to finally get a word in. "That night I told you I didn't see you that way? That was a joke. A stupid, careless joke obviously, but it wasn't supposed to hurt you. I wish you'd let me know that was why you were moving. Given me a sign or a chance to fight for what we have... anything."

"It wasn't a joke to me," Georgie said. She was speaking so quietly Madelyn had to lean in closer to hear.

"And for that I don't think I'll ever be able to apologize enough, G."

Madelyn took Georgie's hand and stroked the back of it, admiring the callused strength of her skin. Though Georgie shrank initially and stiffened as if she were going to withdraw, she let Madelyn keep her hand.

"Ok," said Georgie. Her voice sounded different, oddly strangled, but then Madelyn noticed that Georgie was crying, too. She wasn't sure the last time she'd seen tears on Georgie's face. If ever.

"I'm sorry. I am so, so sorry. I shouldn't have made light of you, because you're the most important person in my entire life. With you in Edmonton, every day is emptier. I wake up wishing you lived here, and I go to sleep wanting to talk to you about what's happened during the day. I get it now, why you needed to leave, but I still wish we'd talked more than just once every few weeks."

"I do too," Georgie said softly.

"And I promise you, not everyone knew that you had feelings for me. Or even that you thought I was sexy enough to bone," Madelyn said. "Hannah and Nadia probably noticed because they're smart, queer people and they know us well. But I know you better than I know myself, and I still couldn't see it. So please don't feel bad."

"You really didn't?" asked Georgie through shaky tears. It almost physically hurt Madelyn to see Georgie so emotional. Her normally stoic composure had loosened to show her deepest fears.

Madelyn shrugged and shook her head. "I missed it. I'm not sure how, but I did. I'm just glad I realized on my own how I felt about you. At least I got that right."

Georgie squeezed Madelyn's hand, then, a renewed energy visibly coursing through her. "Maybe there were better ways to tell me."

"Better places, definitely. Circumstances, one hundred percent yes. But you know it's not every day you get snowed into a cabin in the middle of nowhere with the love of your life."

"Of your life?"

Madelyn kissed Georgie's shoulder, enjoying the soft feeling of the shirt beneath her lips. "My life."

Breathing in deeply, Georgie sat up straighter. "I should have been better too, Mads. All those pictures you sent me yesterday. Everything. It reminded me that I've been short-changing our friendship because I was so scared you'd realize I loved you. And cutting things off when I moved hurt me. It hurt you, too, but I think it hurt me even more."

"So I wasn't crazy to send all those texts even though you weren't responding?"

Georgie laughed, throwing her head back in glee. "Oh no, you were completely nuts. But it was nuts in just the right way. Madelyn nuts, the only kind of nuts I want in my life."

"Did you really just make a testicle joke while we're both sitting here crying together?"

"Would I even be myself if I didn't try to avoid my feelings however I can?"

"Good point."

They sat for a spell, enjoying the touch of each other's skin. Their shoulders were pressed against each other and body heat shared the spaces between.

"In case I wasn't clear before, Georgie, I love you and I'm in love with you. I probably have been for a long time before I realized who I was. And I just wanted you to know that before you go on with your life. I'm sorry our timing didn't match up."

"I love you, too, Madelyn. That's what I came here to say. Well, that and that I'm sorry for bailing out of shame."

"So you do still... there's still hope for..." Madelyn started several fresh sentences but couldn't stick with any of them. Her heart was racing too fast, mind too focused on squealing with excitement. "Oh thank god."

With a shaky smile, the two stared at each other. Georgie's hair was mussed into an endearing cowlick, while Madelyn's red-rimmed eyes made her look haunted with emotion. They hadn't been prepared for where their friendship would lead.

At least now, they had each other for support again.

"Would you mind if I kissed you?" asked Georgie.

"Ever the gentleman, G," Madelyn laughed shakily.

"Is that a yes?"

"Fuck yes," said Madelyn. And she closed the distance between them eagerly, welcoming Georgie's tear-salted lips against her own.

Where their kiss in the cabin had been tumultuous, breaking long-held silences and uncomfortable secrets, this one was full of renewal. It healed as much as it heated them.

Madelyn's thoughts dissolved, leaving behind only traces of how upset she'd been. She relished the sweet and salty taste of Georgie's lips and then let her own part to allow Georgie's tongue access to her mouth.

The kiss deepened in stages: first with tongues entwined, playfully tasting each other and jockeying for dominance. Georgie then cupped Madelyn's neck with her right hand, pulling her closer. And just as Madelyn was sure this was the best she'd ever felt kissing anyone, it got better.

Sparks tingled along the back of Madelyn's neck down

her spine, joining whispers of perfect bliss that shot from her core along the sides of her ribcage. Madelyn's entire body was stirred by the kiss, to speak nothing of her mind.

She was happy. For the first time in months, years, fully happy. And it wasn't from her stupid plan, or because she'd jumped over herself to do the big, romantic gesture with Georgie. It was from being honest, making herself vulnerable, and hoping against all rational thought that Georgie would do the same.

Georgie began to kiss Madelyn down the side of her cheek to the soft skin of her throat, following a path down her collarbone and further. She pushed Madelyn's sweater aside and then tugged it free from her waistband so that she could take the garment off entirely. While Madelyn raised her arms, Georgie lifted the sweater up and freed her.

She'd been working at home, so she wasn't wearing anything special. Just a well-worn white tank top underneath an old sweater, her breasts barely supported by the built-in bra. As Georgie appreciated the view, Madelyn felt her nipples prick against the fabric, raising up beneath the attention.

"I didn't get a chance to say before," Georgie whispered, "but you're beautiful."

Madelyn wasn't normally self-conscious. She was accustomed to making odd statements and cringing sometimes, yes, but she mostly interacted with the world at face value. With Georgie staring at her like she wanted to make her scream louder than the concrete apartment walls could muffle, her face warmed red hot.

"And you're sexy," she responded. It felt right, despite how cheesy the words made her feel. With Georgie, she wanted to keep saying exactly what she wanted when she wanted to.

Enough with keeping things in. Enough hiding and uncertainty. They'd finally discovered how they'd actually felt, for so long, and Madelyn wanted to revel in it.

She unbuttoned Georgie's shirt slowly, staring deeply into Georgie's eyes as she moved. It may well have been the most erotic dance in the world for how arresting it felt. Madelyn's breath hitched when she finally freed Georgie from the shirt entirely, and she dove to the smooth, firm abs beneath.

While Madelyn nipped at Georgie's stomach with a hunger that surprised them both, Georgie took off her bralette and then leaned back to enjoy the view. Tendrils of Madelyn's sandy hair encircled her, while the afternoon sunshine streaming through the blind slats dappled them with light.

"Was this what you'd hoped would happen?" Madelyn asked, surfacing from her work.

"Way more than I could ever have dreamed of, Mads. I mean, sure, I've fantasized. I've had dreams. But I never really thought you would actually want me back."

Madelyn grinned at Georgie, whose sincerity shone from her deep-set eyes. "Guess what, though: I do!"

And with a happy yelp, she tackled Georgie, the two of them rolling sideways on the floor before landing with Madelyn on her back.

They kissed until it felt like some sequel version of high school, where making out was a valued and well-worn activity. It could have been minutes or hours that passed, the sun sinking lower behind the apartment blinds the only sign that time had elapsed.

"Georgie," she said, pulling back from another kiss. "I want you."

Without another word, they got up from their revelry

and shed the rest of their clothes. It was a quiet minute, maybe two, and then Madelyn led Georgie to the soft sheets of her bed, sinking deep beneath the comforter so that they could enjoy themselves together.

She didn't need anything but this: Georgie, a comfortable bed, and the prospect of pizza sometime after their energy had been spent.

Madelyn should have had more faith in her friend, but the journey they had just been on brought them closer, despite the twists and turns. Wherever the future might bring them, at least they'd bridged that first, most painful gap.

The rest was just details.

18

"HARDER!" MADELYN GASPED, THE WORD ESCAPING HER LIKE A hiss of hot steam. She felt like she was boiling. Georgie shook Madelyn with deft thrusts from her strap-on. Each of Georgie's hands made a deep imprint on Madelyn's hips from behind.

Georgie obliged Madelyn's moaned instructions and gripped harder, moved faster and deeper, each thrust punctuating Madelyn's mind with a new level of pleasure. She was making noises she didn't recognize now, pure blissful animalistic noises.

Madelyn was close to ecstasy, but Georgie hastened the trajectory by reaching around past her hips and playing with her deftly. As Madelyn's hips bucked at the attention, a new sound erupted from her mouth.

Hips moving, muscles clenching, body completely dazzled by the sensation, Madelyn collapsed onto her stomach on the bed. Georgie laughed as she buckled on top of Madelyn, rolling to the side quickly so as not to hurt her.

"Holy fuck, G. I have never felt that good in my entire life."

Georgie smirked. "Challenge accepted. Let's see if we can beat that tomorrow."

"Really?" said Madelyn, raising an eyebrow. "What part of you heard the noise I just made and thought 'needs work'?"

"Don't get me wrong, Mads. I liked it. Loved it. But isn't life about chasing the best of what we can do? I'm just saying, I think I can do better."

"Better than me?" Madelyn pouted, stroking the beads of sweat from Georgie's chest.

"No, better than my personal best. Making you scream like a hyena being physically assaulted by a tourist."

Madelyn laughed but felt guilty for having done so. "That's... dark."

Georgie shrugged and just kept smiling. "Part of the package. I might be good in bed, but I'm less good at metaphors."

"Similes."

"Hm?" said Georgie, as if Madelyn had stuttered.

"You said 'like a hyena' so it's a simile. Metaphors claim the thing actually is the thing, not *like* the thing."

"Ok, I'm going to trust you on that one. You've got the book smarts and I'll be the street smarts."

"Does welding really count as street smart? Like if someone mugged you, being able to weld your way out of the situation would be helpful?"

Georgie snorted, raising herself up on an elbow to look Madelyn over. Nakedness stretched before her gaze and Madelyn felt lovingly admired. "You are too smart for your own good, Mads. Welding's closer to street smarts than history is."

"Maybe on some streets, but I guarantee that being able

to talk about wartime victory gardens in Alberta would come in handy in certain situations."

"Certain very specific gardening situations. Where there's a time machine."

"Exactly," said Madelyn. She folded her arms and nodded like the matter was fully concluded.

They hadn't left her apartment in a couple days, having completely nested: several pizza boxes were stacked in the to-be-composted bucket near her recycling and Georgie had had to resort to borrowed clothing, none of which suited her.

"When are we going to face reality?" Georgie said after a pause. "I love this, doing this, but I don't have infinite days to take off work."

"Term starts back up on Monday, too."

"Where does that leave us?"

Madelyn tied her hair up in a messy ponytail, stalling for time. "Where do you want it to leave us?"

"You are so noncommittal sometimes, Madelyn."

"Blame it on my Libra sun," laughed Madelyn. "It's having too much fun with you. I don't want it to end."

"Neither do I. But I also can't bring myself to blame it on anything but hormones and feelings. The stars have nothing to do with it."

"Exactly what a Cap would say."

"Ha ha. Seriously, though." Georgie was staring at Madelyn with the intensity of someone wise beyond their years.

"Blah. Do we have to?"

"I think it's a good idea. We love each other. We live in two different places. How are we going to bridge that gap?"

"Well," said Madelyn, picking at the end of her ponytail. "I'm loaded up with teaching commitments this term. But next year, maybe, I could go anywhere. At least in theory. My advisor has a few students who work on their dissertations from small towns or other cities."

"I don't get a ton of vacation, but I could try to come down here on weekends. Or we could alternate?"

"If I'm hearing you right, it sounds like we're both thinking the same thing..." Madelyn didn't want to say it out loud. The idea was still such a commitment, a potentially serious endeavor.

"Which is?" asked Georgie. Madelyn should have predicted that her friend would be the shyer one about this conversation. It had, after all, taken her years to come to terms with her feelings. Why would her pace suddenly quicken?

"We should try to make this work. Long distance."

It hadn't been clear to Madelyn whether Georgie was in fact thinking the same thing as her, but any doubt was immediately vanquished by the smile that grew on Georgie's face.

"You really think so?"

"I wouldn't deplete my electrolytes so badly for anyone else, G." Madelyn waved an empty Gatorade bottle at Georgie, one of several she'd resorted to after their multi-day love fest.

"What if it makes you resent me?" asked Georgie. Her expression was plaintive, vulnerable. Madelyn had rarely seen her look that way before. It had been a transformative few days.

"Hey, I resented you for moving to Edmonton this past year and look where that's taken us."

Georgie grimaced and swatted at Madelyn's thigh.

"What if we can't figure out a way to close the distance?"

"Like I said earlier, my program only has a residency

requirement for the first bit. Then we can talk. Also, that's a problem for future Georgie and Mads."

"And what if it ruins our friendship?"

Madelyn took a deep breath, her gut acknowledging that this was her biggest fear all along. And yet, here they were. "What if it doesn't? What if everything goes amazingly and we're super happy with our choices? What if we fall deeply in love, get married, and live happily ever after? What then?"

"What-ifs don't sound so realistic when they're happy, I guess." The slant of Georgie's mouth told Madelyn that she wasn't buying this optimism.

"Given that we just went through the biggest risks to our friendship since we first met, I think I'm willing to gamble."

Despite the confidence Madelyn projected in her voice, she was still uneasy beneath the surface. Georgie had never been an easy sell on sunny outlooks. Toughness and grit, she understood. Having hope? Less so.

But Madelyn wanted to put all her feelings out there, to demonstrate that she was all in. Because she was and saying anything else would be a self-preserving lie.

"Are you?" she asked Georgie.

The longest pause of Madelyn's life transpired. And when Madelyn wasn't sure she could last any longer, Georgie spoke.

"I am."

A few days later, with Georgie on the road back up North, Madelyn sat at her computer. Editing had been slow going before, but today she found herself miraculously unblocked. The last few changes no longer seemed insurmountable, and new words flowed from her like they'd been waiting eagerly to be committed to a document.

She finished the latest draft with a smile on her face, surprised at the confidence she now felt. Providing they weren't too angry with her late revisions, this paper was going to be accepted. She would have her first publication.

With this newfound confidence, Madelyn opened her university email account to check what had happened while she was on break. In amongst the automated university notifications and the late requests for extensions she had already addressed before leaving for Banff, she saw an unread email.

It was from the student whose grandmother was dying.

"Dear Prof. Melnyk,

Thank you so much for being understanding about my late paper. My grandma died a few days ago, but I was able to make it to the hospital to be with her before she passed. I want you to know how much that means to me."

Attached was a selfie taken by the student with her grandmother. The elderly woman was smiling though clearly ill in bed, her thin hand clasping that of her granddaughter. Madelyn dissolved into tears.

It had been a difficult Christmas this year, but she was glad to have gone through it. Whatever might happen this term, or this year, she'd made huge steps towards getting what she wanted out of life.

Madelyn often felt buffeted by her intuition, thinking it a flighty, unreliable voice of temptation bent on making her choices weak and selfish. But this year, she'd listened.

And it had been the best decision she'd ever made.

EPILOGUE

One Year Later

"Did you pack the beer?" asked Madelyn. Georgie huffed and pointed towards the opened back of the truck, where several cases of beer were visible. "Oh. Thank you!"

"We're going to be late," Georgie said. She waited as Madelyn fussed over a selection of bags of chips, pondering which ones to bring. "And they have chips in Banff. We can get more if we run out."

"But we bought these just for the trip," Madelyn sighed, turning away from the pile on the driveway to grab Georgie's hand. "I can't waste them."

"Trust me, they won't be wasted here. When I come back from the cabin, I'll be sure to eat them all after work one day."

"As long as they find a good home."

"My stomach, and then eventually the toilet," said Georgie. She laughed at the grimace Madelyn made and then slammed the truck's tailgate shut. Madelyn had driven up to Edmonton to spend a few days with Georgie before the cabin trip. Georgie's rented room in the suburban house had felt more like home those few days than any of the previous year.

It had been almost exactly a year since they'd started officially dating. Time had flown. But it turns out time always flies when you've got almost every weekend booked solid with travel.

Alternating between Calgary and Edmonton for months on end had been exhausting, though welcome. For the next five days, they'd be staying in the same place, no long-distance trips required of each other. And the best part was that they got to do the journey together.

"Thanks again for driving up here so we could head to Banff together, Mads."

Madelyn hugged Georgie from behind and kissed her neck, inhaling deeply afterwards to take in Georgie's warm, spicy scent. "Anytime."

"We ready?"

"I think so," said Madelyn, her eyes darting to the house one last time as if there had been something left behind she urgently needed to spot. She was nervous but couldn't tell Georgie why.

"That's good enough for me. Let's haul ass."

Georgie's crude turn of phrase snapped Madelyn out of her contemplative mood and made her burst out laughing. "Onwards, Captain!"

They piled into Georgie's truck and backed out of the driveway, leaving Madelyn's car parked in Georgie's roommate's spot. He'd be out of town for another two weeks' rotation up in the oil patch.

"Did you make that playlist you were talking about?" asked Georgie.

"I diiiid!" Madelyn eagerly reached for her phone and

plugged in the auxiliary cable, doing a celebratory dance as the first song started playing.

"Oh no. Madelyn, no. Did you seriously put a song from MuchDance Mix '99 on here?"

"'A' song? What makes you think the playlist isn't just MuchDance Mix?"

Georgie shot Madelyn a wide-eyed, horrified look. "No."

"Just kidding. I wouldn't do that to you. But you should have seen how you looked!"

"I'll keep my eyes on the road, thanks. And once you've had your fun with this mix, don't worry. There's plenty of punk to clean out your ears when we're done."

"My ears are squeaky clean, thanks." Madelyn grinned at Georgie as they pulled onto the arterial road that would lead them to the highway. Only a few more hours until she'd do it.

"Guess I'll have to dirty them up later tonight, then." Georgie shot Madelyn a smoldering look and Madelyn felt heat rise up her neck. Eagerness to enjoy each other's bodies while on vacation ran into a barrier.

"I'd love that. But... you remember that Nadia and Hannah will already be there, right?"

Though Georgie paused, it was almost imperceptible. "I do. And that's ok. They've seen worse before, right?"

Madelyn smiled. "Right."

Georgie had finally gotten over her barriers about PDA around friends. Sure, they'd all hung out a bunch in Calgary when Georgie was in town, but that was different. This week, they'd be sleeping in close quarters with the people by whom Georgie had felt so scrutinized. It loosened some of Madelyn's anticipatory tension to see how much more secure Georgie was, even now.

"I love you," she said, reaching over to squeeze Georgie's

thigh. The affectionate gesture was familiar and exhilarating in equal parts.

"I love *you*, Madelyn." Georgie smiled at Madelyn and then honked the horn of her truck.

"Hey! What was that for?" shrieked Madelyn. A Toyota driver to their left on the highway glanced over in defensive shock at the sound.

"Just telling the world how I feel."

"With...honking?"

"Fuck yes!" said Georgie, moving her hand as if to honk the horn again, but Madelyn stopped her.

"No, don't cause an accident! There's too much traffic."

"Sometimes it's too easy to tease you, Mads." Georgie smirked at Madelyn with a devastating glint to her eye. "Like now."

"Fine, fine," Madelyn said, shrugging with a resigned smile. She then turned the volume of the music up much, much louder and raised her eyebrows at Georgie. "You've got your weak spots, too, hey?"

And so, they drove along the wintry highway towards their vacation spot, happily bickering in the way couples do —with hearts full of affection and an intimate understanding of how best to push buttons.

Nadia had been responsible for booking the cabin this time, and she'd chosen a spot much less secluded than the previous year. Better safe than sorry. When Georgie and Madelyn reached the cabin driveway, they parked in the visitor lot for the condo complex. It would take a few trips to unload their gear, but that was ok. The walk from the lot to the front door took them along a beautiful woodsy pathway. Very romantic.

Madelyn had planned it all out.

She fiddled with the packet in her right-hand pocket and nearly lost her courage. Georgie had already started unloading groceries and bags, though, so Madelyn slid out of her seat and onto the snowy ground.

"Leave that last bag for me," she said brightly. Grabbing its handles, she pulled it off the truck and walked alongside a heavily laden Georgie to the front door. A few other things were already piled there from Georgie's previous trips back and forth.

"That didn't take long," said Madelyn. Her voice sounded strained and falsely bright, so she took a deep breath.

She was nervous.

Georgie pressed the button on her key fob to lock the truck remotely and the vehicle honked in response.

Just as Georgie was about to ring up to the others to let them in, Madelyn spoke.

"Wait, I think I forgot something."

She thought she heard Georgie sigh in frustration, but Madelyn was too keyed-up to be hurt.

"Can you come back with me for a sec?" she asked. Georgie nodded briskly and jangled her keys while they walked back along the path. The waning daylight made the snow crystals sparkle like magic. Madelyn paused by the rough-hewn wooden bench she'd seen along the pathway.

She sat down and gestured for Georgie to join her.

"Shouldn't leave those things by the front for too long. Don't want someone to take them," said Georgie. Madelyn nodded, the words barely sinking in.

"Georgie," said Madelyn. She resisted the urge to fiddle with the packet again. "Isn't it amazing that it's already been a year since last trip's mess?"

"Time flies," nodded Georgie. She rubbed her hands together impatiently and glanced back towards the condo.

"It may have only been a year, but it's been the best year of my life."

"You're sweet, Mads. Let's talk about this more inside."

"Just wait—I won't be long." Madelyn smiled at Georgie's hurried, tapping foot and reached into the pocket where she'd kept the ring.

Georgie's mouth dropped open, and she laughed a single, staccato burst.

"Georgie, will you marry me?" asked Madelyn, sinking to her knee on the sidewalk. The cement was cold beneath her jeans but she felt impervious to discomfort. Too much adrenaline flooded her.

"Of course I'll marry you," Georgie said, grinning. "That ring for me?"

"Who else would it be for?" said Madelyn, holding up the piece of jewelry in her mitten. Though Georgie took it, she shoved it on her finger with a less delicate motion than many brides might.

"Guess I might have to take better care of my nails if everyone wants to see this ring all the time now."

"It looks good on you," said Madelyn, standing up from her kneeling position. She tilted Georgie's chin upwards so she could kiss her. "Future wife."

"Ok, now we have to get inside." Georgie spoke abruptly, standing and starting the walk towards the condo before Madelyn could say anything. "I'm guessing you didn't actually forget anything?"

Though happiness still soared in her–she'd just gotten engaged to the love of her life, after all—Madelyn's feelings began to sink. Georgie was acting weird. "No, nothing forgotten."

She followed Georgie to the condo entrance and up the elevator to their rental unit. The bags and gear took a little maneuvering, and by the time they'd reached the actual front door to the condo, Madelyn was outright annoyed.

Why couldn't Georgie act a little more joyful about this?

Georgie knocked, smiling briefly back at Madelyn with a strange expression. The deadbolt slid shortly afterward and Nadia answered the door.

"You're here!" she exclaimed in a voice too loud for the occasion.

"Hey! So we've got these bags to take in, but you'll never guess–" Madelyn started to say, bubbling over with eagerness to share their happy news.

"Just a sec, Mads," said Georgie. She shot Madelyn a glance that said 'cool it.' Hurt dampened the last of Madelyn's post-proposal jitters and she fought to stay smiling.

They pushed their things inside and closed the door, and then Georgie took Madelyn's hand. Madelyn almost didn't want to let her, but she relented. Even if she were a little hurt by Georgie's strange reactions, she still loved her.

They were still going to be married.

As Nadia led them down the entranceway's hall and into the main living area of the condo, Madelyn fought the sadness piercing through her otherwise blissful evening.

"Oh!" she said, involuntarily, when they reached the living room. Hannah and Nadia turned to smile at Georgie and Madelyn, surrounded by a group of familiar faces. Most of Georgie and Madelyn's friends were there, along with

Sasha, Mila, Ariel, and a good contingent of Georgie's family. "What's going on?"

A bunting banner was strung across the far wall with triangles bearing felted letters that spelled out MADELYN. Before she could say anything else about the surprise, Madelyn gasped again when Nadia, Hannah, Ariel, and Sasha held up signs that read "Will," "You," "Marry," and "Me?"

Shock nearly paralyzed Madelyn, but she heard Georgie clear her throat and say her name. So she turned, as if in slow motion, and came to face her love, who knelt right next to her with a small velvet box held up in her hands.

Madelyn's tears flowed swiftly, springing up out of the heartfelt surprise so suddenly that she barely bore witness to the ring Georgie offered her. Emotion overwhelmed her.

"Mads, you're my favorite person. I want to spend my life with you."

"Yes!" yelped Madelyn ecstatically.

The hush of the waiting crowd murmured with laughter when Georgie widened her eyes. "I haven't even finished yet," she said.

Tears began to stream down Georgie's face, too, and Madelyn barely knew how to string together a sentence. She'd been wracked with anxiety about her own proposal, so consumed by it that apparently she'd missed the signs that Georgie was planning one too.

"My answer's yes, though," said Madelyn. "Just like yours was."

"Hm?" Madelyn heard Nadia mutter to Hannah.

And then Madelyn's teary joy overflowed into laughter, a belly-shaking, all-consuming form of it that she couldn't contain. Georgie managed to slide the ring onto Madelyn's finger while she kept on giggling, and the two stood, hand in hand, to present themselves to the group.

They were engaged—twice now.

With this presentation complete, their friends and family clapped, cheered, and whistled. If Madelyn had thought she was overwhelmed with feeling before, this outpouring of support added a new layer of intensity to the mix.

Hannah brought Prosecco to Georgie and Madelyn while Nadia insisted on taking pictures as they clinked their glasses together.

"What the hell, G. I thought you were embarrassed by everyone knowing your feelings. That's why I wanted to propose in private, all alone."

Georgie snorted with laughter and sipped her drink. Nodding, she answered: "Yeah, I realized I was guarding myself too much. Why shouldn't the people closest to us know we're in love and happy together? You deserve to be showered in as much love as is humanly possible."

Ariel, who stood nearby, her mane of golden hair impeccably styled, overheard their exchange. "You two are too much!"

"A toast!" cried out another friend. While the hubbub showed no signs of dying down, Madelyn drank her Prosecco, Georgie's hand firmly grasped in her own. The celebrations unfolded around them, loved ones genuinely happy to see the two of them together.

"Thank you," said Madelyn to Georgie. "It was perfect."

Georgie grinned and stood up straighter than Madelyn had ever seen. "So was yours, Mads. I'm glad we had your proposal all on our own."

Then she set down her glass on a nearby end table, taking Madelyn's drink from her smoothly before wrapping her into a deep, low-bending kiss. While the gathered crowd cheered and laughed and applauded their love, Madelyn's heart pounded with the absolute, earth-shaking certainty that this was precisely how things should have unfolded.

She wouldn't change a thing.

AUTHOR'S NOTE

Hello! Thank you for reading *Never Just Friends.*

As I sit down to write this note, it's currently -40 outside. (Fun fact: this is the point where Celsius and Fahrenheit converge, so it's the same number in both systems). Winter in Canada can be no joke.

Rather than dwell on the downsides of the season, I wanted to channel everything I loved about winter into this book: the quiet, the sense of intimacy, the slower pace of things when the world outside is hushed and frozen. Though it's a time when the days are short and darkness never seems far away, it's also a season of growing closer and sharing small joys with the people you love.

I wrote Georgie and Madelyn's story to convey as much as I could of those feelings. I hope you liked it.

Indie authors like myself benefit greatly from reviews, so please consider leaving a review on Amazon or Goodreads if you have the time.

And if you'd like to hear from me when I have new books out, sign up for my mailing list. I get in touch no more than once a month, so I promise your inbox will remain uncluttered (at least by me!): http://eepurl.com/dhf1Vz

If you'd like to hear more about my day-to-day writing life, which of course involves a fair portion of procrastination and pictures of my cat, follow me on Twitter:

http://twitter.com/authorlilycraig

ALSO BY LILY CRAIG

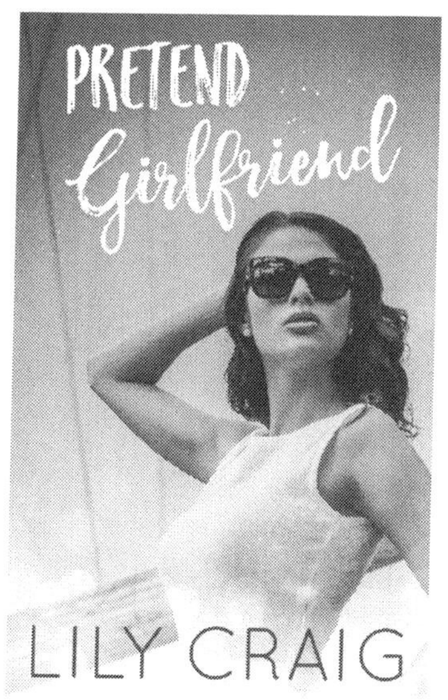

Pretend Girlfriend ~ Available on Amazon

Fake love, real sparks.

When Celeste Lamontagne receives a wedding invitation from her ex, she's furious. The only thing worse than being cheated on? Seeing your ex and the girl she cheated with get married. Less than a year later. And as part of a two-week long Mediterranean cruise. But they say the best revenge is a life well lived, right? Not for Celeste, it isn't. It's arranging an elaborate fake relationship with someone to make your ex jealous.

Lane Bishop is the perfect someone to do just that. Impulsive to the extreme, she loses her job right in front of Celeste. There goes Lane's best shot at becoming a stylist in New York City. She can have another chance if she agrees to travel with Celeste, pretending to be her girlfriend so that Celeste's ex sees her happy and thriving. The only catch? Celeste's an heiress accustomed to getting everything she wants. She's rigorous about details—some might say spoiled—which clashes with a free spirit like Lane.

Two weeks travelling in close quarters challenges the faux lovebirds. They've got to appear harmoniously in love, even when they'd rather rib each other than whisper sweet nothings. But the sparks between Celeste and Lane become harder and harder to ignore. Can they convince the wedding guests of their passion without the flames setting them both alight?

Listing Date ~ Available on Amazon

Skye's plan is simple: craft the perfect life. Move back to her hometown of Toronto, Canada after years working in the U.S. tech scene. Start a new job as a C-level executive at one of the world's best fertility apps. Get pregnant on her own and raise her kids happily ever after. Easy. Except when Skye arrives home, she discovers Toronto's real estate market is more difficult to navigate than she thought.

Penny has always wanted to own her own business, so she took a leap of faith. Now she's a realtor struggling to launch her fledgling firm. When Skye walks into an open house Penny's running, Penny sees her chance to soar and takes it. How hard could it be to find the perfect home for someone as impressively organized as Skye?

When Penny's sunny optimism meets Skye's hyper-logical life plan, the two women find that life is often what happens between the lines of your to-do list.

Gal Pals ~ Available on Amazon

Hollywood starlet Vanessa Corrington reached a new level of fame last year: a blockbuster hit with sequels slated, award show buzz, and countless rave reviews. Her life should be perfect, but something's missing. Though she's never deliberately concealed her sexuality, she's also never dated anyone since landing her first job in Los Angeles.

So when Tara, a free spirited photographer, snaps Vanessa's picture—and accidentally lands her squarely in the sights of a group of paparazzi–Vanessa isn't sure what to think. Tara's cute, yes. Interested, probably. And their chemistry is undeniable.

But is Vanessa willing to risk her personal life showing up in the public eye when she's normally gone to such pains to keep it private?

In Her Eyes ~ Available on Amazon

College freshman Danica has her hands full with anxiety. At least that's what she tells herself when she wonders why she hasn't dated since arriving at McEown College. Then a stunning, sultry woman walks into her figure drawing class and sheds her clothes. Suddenly, Danica's thinking about anything but academics...

Bailey's modeled for art classes on campus dozens of times, but there's something different about the girl with the short hair who's blushing like a fiend, who can't meet Bailey's eye even while she's supposed to be drawing her. Danica's way too shy for Bailey's tastes, but even a shy girl could use a social circle.

As Danica befriends Bailey and her group of third-year pals, the sparks between them become harder to ignore. Commitment isn't exactly Bailey's forte, but with Danica she's starting to think she might be willing to take the chance.

Made in the USA
Middletown, DE
01 May 2019